HAVE YOU SEEN CHARLIE?

———————

K. H. BROCKWELL

Have You Seen Charlie

Published by Plume Serpent Publishing

Summary: There are some people who are destined to change the world- and there is one dog who is destined to find them. When a Los Alamos scientist is on the verge of completing a world-changing project and finds a drowning puppy in the Rio Grande her entire world is changed forever.

ISBN 978-0615591193

Fiction

Dedication

Dedicated to my four legged companions. My life would not be the same without them.

Special thanks to: my husband and my children for supporting me in this endeavor.

Table of Contents

Meet the Press

It seemed as though I had been waiting for this day my entire life. "What will I say, how will I dress, what will people think and will there be any more surprises? None of these questions will be answered if I don't get out of bed, but if I get out of bed then I'll have to answer all of them." Motionless under the covers, I pretended to be asleep. I wondered, "Do I get up and face the day or do I will myself to die in my sleep?" Realizing the latter was difficult to achieve, and a much more permanent condition, I slowly opened my eyes.

Opening my eyes was Charlie's cue to pounce. Every morning this was our routine. Charlie knew the exact moment my eyes opened which, in his mind, was implied permission to jump on my chest and lick my face and ears. His timing was impeccable and once I was awake he was relentless with his demands.

"Good morning to you too, Charlie. Yes, I know you need to go outside and yes, I know it is time for breakfast. One thing at a time boy, one thing at a time."

There is a certain humility that comes from owning a dog. No matter how important you become or how high your level of prestige, to your dog, you are and will always be, the person who answers to them. I have fantasized about being reincarnated as a dog. What a wonderful life it must be. My every need met, never worrying about money or a job, unconditional love, it sounds great to me.

With the biggest day of my life looming, my first order of business for the day was dealing with Charlie's first order of business. Once the morning pleasantries were concluded, it was time for coffee, shower and breakfast. I switched on the iPod so Charlie and I could have some music while I made my coffee, and his breakfast.

I have what I refer to as a psychic iPod. I leave it on "shuffle," and somehow it always seems to play the perfect song at the perfect time. Sometimes the "perfect" song is interesting or often humorous but on this occasion it was little alarming. The first song of the day was "The Winner," by Bobby Bare. I stood fixed staring at the iPod. I tried to decide if I should be reassured by the title or horrified by the lyrics. "The Winner" is a song about getting exactly what you asked for, but probably not exactly what you wanted.

"Well, I am a winner," I reassured myself. "It's just a stupid song."

With Bobby Bare's voice wafting through the kitchen, I sat down with my first of many cups of coffee for the day.

My phone vibrating across the countertop interrupted my internal conversation. Instinctively I checked the caller ID. "DAD" was flashing with each ring.

"Charlie, it's your grandpa! Do you want to talk?" Charlie barked with excitement.

"Okay then, you say 'hello'". I pressed the speaker button and Charlie greeted Dad with a very enthusiastic "hello!"

"Good morning Charlie, is your Mom around?" I heard Dad say.

"Yeah, Dad I'm here. What's up?"

"What time should I pick up Charlie?"

"The press conference is at two, but I have to meet Joe at noon. He is sending a stylist over at ten to make sure I'm presentable. God, I hate this. Why can't I just issue a news bulletin? 'Scientist's discovery to save planet, details at eleven.' That would be so much simpler."

"Simple is not what you do. So, do you want to keep Charlie to chase the stylist off or should I be there before ten?"

"Oh how I wish Charlie was an attack dog. You know he'll just lick her to death. Since that won't deter her much, how about heading over after you finish your breakfast? I should be out of the shower by then, if I get off the phone."

"Okay, I'll see you in a little while. Bye Charlie, Grandpa will come take you to the park and then we'll get some ice cream. I know your Mom loves it when I feed you ice cream."

"Really, Dad! You know ice cream gives him gas. That's how you treat someone you love? I would really hate to be your enemy."

"Now that I have you good and humble, I'll see you soon. Love ya kid."

"Love you too Dad and no ice cream for either of you."

I finished another cup of coffee and headed off to the shower. Willie was drowning in a "Whiskey River" on the iPod, which seemed like a real good idea at that moment. I considered spiking my coffee on my way to the shower but decided against a dose of liquid courage. Today I would need a clear mind and a sharp wit. I had a new bottle of Blanton's, but it would have to wait until our post announcement celebration.

I enjoyed a long hot shower with Charlie guarding the door. I've tried to explain to him that there is only one way in and out of the bathroom. I can't go in and disappear, but he wants to make sure. So the door must stay open and he lays half in and half out of the doorway, ensuring no one can enter or exit without his knowledge. By the time I was done with my shower, the steam had collected on Charlie like the morning dew. Tiny little droplets of water sat on his silver eyelashes and black ears. His coat sparkled in the morning sun while he waited patiently for me to finish my morning routine. Before I could leave the bathroom he gave my calf a quick lick to check my lotion.

"Let's go Charlie. We need to pick the proper outfit for today. I really wish getting dressed was as easy for me as it is for you. No one ever says, 'Charlie, didn't you have that fur on the last time I saw you?'"

Charlie gave his coat a good shake to rid himself of the steam and broke into his puppy routine. Tail wagging, butt up, paws out flat, next thing I knew, there he went off with my towel.

"Hey that's rude," I yelled.

I was standing naked in the hall when I heard Dad come in the back door.

"Shit! Dad, please stay in the kitchen! Charlie took my towel. I'll be there in a minute."

As I streaked to my room I could hear Dad congratulating Charlie on putting me in my place.

"Good boy Charlie. That'll teach her to cut us off from the Good Humor man."

"You know I can hear you? I have no idea what sin I must have committed, the penance for which is sharing my life with the two of you overgrown children!" I bellowed down the hall while jumping into my sweats.

"Charlie, just ignore her, she's using her big words which means she's stressed. Let's get your leash and leave the evil queen to her bidding."

"Nice, I'm left naked in the hall by Charlie and you think I'm evil? Really!"

I reconsidered spiking my coffee as I left my room and went into the kitchen.

"Insults aside Dad, thanks for taking Charlie. Today is going to be hectic at the very least and I don't need to be worried about him. I'll call you in the morning and take you both to the dog park. I'll even stop and get your favorite breakfast burritos on the way. We'll talk about everything while Charlie burns off all the treats I know you're going to feed him."

"Taking Charlie is my pleasure. We always enjoy each other's company. You know, male bonding stuff. Good luck today. Promise you won't forget the little people once you're a household name and promise to stay safe."

"I promise. I love both of you. Now get out of my kitchen so I can get ready."

I poured myself another cup of coffee as I watched Dad and Charlie drive away.

My next task of the morning was getting some clothes ready for the stylist. I needed to have some idea of what I wanted to wear. If I didn't I would end up in a puffy pirate shirt or something equally as awful. I wasn't sure what the correct fashion choice was for my announcement. I thought about deferring to my boots and hat. That was good enough for Dad and Charlie and I thought it should be good enough for the rest of the world but I knew Joe wouldn't allow it. He hated my "cowgirl chic" as he called it. He insisted that my science would never be taken seriously if I ran around looking like the Marlboro Girl. I strongly disagreed but I did trust him when it came to public relations. So I picked out a collection of Santa Fe inspired shirts, skirts, and concho belts and threw in my best black patent leather boots to finish off the look.

"That will just have to be fashionable enough. The stylist can mix and match until she gets something she is satisfied with, but I am not spending today dressed in someone else's clothes." I said to myself.

Just then the doorbell rang.

"Come on in, it's open."

"Good morning Catherine. I'm Chloe and I'll be your stylist for today."

"Great. Sorry, I mean, nice to meet you Chloe. Thanks for coming. Did Joe warn you I'm not exactly a fashionista?"

"Joe may have mentioned something along those lines but I'm sure we can sort you out and have you looking fabulous for your press conference."

"Are people in the fashion world the only ones who actually say fabulous?"

"Soooo, let's see what we have to work with."

Chloe looked over the clothes I had picked out like someone smelling onions. My boots were the only things she seemed to like.

"What else do you have that you're not showing me?"

I knew where this was going and I could feel myself tense up as I opened my closet. She was going to pick something that I should have gotten rid of years ago, something that I hated but for some unknown reason I had not thrown out.

"Oh, see here. This is lovely, and this has some potential, and this…"

God, here we go, just breathe and remember she is good at fashion and you have just changed the world.

A little perspective from my inner voice and suddenly Chloe wasn't nearly as annoying.

After what seemed like an intolerable amount of wardrobe changes, Chloe was happy with an outfit. Next, she tackled my hair and makeup. Makeup is where I draw some very definite lines. I usually don't wear any makeup. I have earned every wrinkle and scar on my face and I don't see any need to cover them up. For the cameras I'll tolerate a little foundation, some shine on my lips and some mascara, but anything else is not going to happen. My hair is usually braided and under my hat so if Joe won't let me wear a hat, Chloe needed to tame my unmanageable mane.

With all my limitations firmly in place, Chloe managed to work her magic and by the time she was done I was well dressed and well coifed. I don't know what Joe paid her, but I she earned every penny.

"Thanks Chloe, you are a true artist."

"It's easy when I have a good base to start from. You do realize you are a very attractive woman?"

"You're too kind Chloe. I have to run, Joe will be waiting for me. Thanks again."

"Just resist the urge to put on your hat or play with your hair and you'll look perfect for your press conference."

"I'll do my best. If we do another one of these I'll be sure Joe calls you."

"Thanks and good luck."

Welcome to Knob Creek

"Charlie, come here!"

A man's voice rang through my ears. My mind was spinning and my head was splitting as I tried to get my eyes to focus on the face just in front of me. Where was I, what had happened? My vision and senses were slowly returning and I realized that I was cold, wet and covered in a blanket.

"That creature is as wanton as a light heeled-wife. It was my fortune to find him in a burlap bag on the banks of the river. He was the only surviving soul of his eight siblings. I roughed his coat, which incited some breathing so I placed him in the pocket of my shirt for warmth. I was unsure of his fate but left unattended he surely would have perished." The man kept rambling on; it was nervous chatter, like he was trying to calm himself.

"Miss, we need to depart this area. Are you able to walk?"

I wasn't really sure. I focused, with all my might on the man hovering over me. His face was thin and drawn and his beard was unkept. It was hard to tell what color it was as it appeared to be coated in tobacco stains. His eyes, it was his eyes that seemed so familiar. They were sky blue with a gray ring. I thought I had seen his eyes before.

"Miss, I must insist, being dilatory may allow for our discovery. Would you permit me to tote you?"

Like a child I reached my arms upward and wrapped my fingers around the strange man's neck. As he stood with me in his arms, I realized how tall and lean he was. He carried me with little effort; his strong sinewy muscles seemed unfazed by my weight. We traveled at a remarkable pace over a considerable distance. Charlie ran along side keeping a watchful eye over us. Finally we arrived at a small cabin set in amongst the pine trees alongside a small creek. Behind the cabin there was a corral and a barn.

The cabin was no bigger than most kitchens, no windows, just a few slits cut in the log walls. Inside, there was a small bed along one wall and a pot bellied wood stove in the center of the back wall. The third wall seemed to be the kitchen with cast iron pans on the wall and a washbasin. There were two wooden chairs in front of the wood stove. The man placed me gently in one of them and started building a fire.

As he worked on the fire, I realized my senses had mostly returned. I started taking inventory of myself and my situation. I was chilled to the bone and wrapped in a wool blanket. I was barefoot. Well, actually I was completely bare under the wool blanket. My hair had an odd odor, like it had been singed. My arms and legs had several cuts and scrapes but I didn't appear to have any significant injuries. My head still hurt and there was a faint ringing in my ears. I felt my scalp and found a fairly deep wound. I sat shivering on the wooden chair trying to understand what had happened. Without realizing it I had started to cry.

Charlie came over and put his head in my lap. He sat right on top of my bare feet and leaned into me.

"Good dog," I whispered.

"You do have the capacity for speech," the man commented as he turned from the stove where he had built a roaring fire.

"Draw close to the stove to warm yourself. I will fetch some habiliments. I have only a tow shirt, overalls and a single pair of silk and oakum stockings to offer. I regret I am unable to provide proper attire for a lady."

"Thanks?"

"I would like to confess I averted my eyes to protect your modesty at the river. I was returning from an ailing neighbor whom I had taken a shoat wrapped in that blanket. I feel fortunate that it was I that found you, not some rouge that may have brought harm upon you. My curious nature does question how it is you came to be along the riverbank in such an unfortunate condition. Did you suffer the misfortune of an attack or merely fall in the river?"

"I fell in the river?"

I really had no idea but since I was naked, cold and wet that seemed like the most plausible explanation. The part I was having trouble with was, why did this man seem so familiar, yet everything else seemed so odd and out of place. One of the most confusing things was the river. The last thing I remember, I was in New Mexico. The closest large river was the Rio Grande. Although I didn't know where I was, I did know the river I had just come out of was not the Rio Grande.

The stranger returned with a linen shirt, a pair of trousers and some socks. I graciously accepted them and while he went out to find us something for dinner I got dressed. I put on the shirt, trousers and socks then covered everything with the wool blanket. It wasn't exactly fashionable but it was warm. My mind was still spinning. My head hurt and I couldn't resist lying down on the bed. I don't know when the man returned because I was fast asleep in his bed. The kind soul spent the night sleeping in a wooden chair in front of the stove.

I awoke to the smell of bacon and eggs, which was my first realization I was starved. My new friend was just finishing his breakfast and he had a plate waiting for me by the stove.

"Thank you," I stammered.

"I felt you must be famished. You had fallen into a deep sleep before my return last evening."

"I'm really sorry for helping myself to your bed. I think I must have been in shock."

"I am not sure I understand, but it would not have been proper for you to sleep in any other location than the bed."

"I'm sorry but I don't remember if you told me your name"

The man stood up, took off his hat and introduced himself.

"My given name is Abraham, or to those familiar with me Abe. Abe Lincoln."

To the glee of Charlie I dropped my plate of bacon and eggs. While Charlie made short work of cleaning up my breakfast I tried to gather myself.

"I'm sorry did you say Abraham Lincoln?"

"Yes, Miss have you taken ill? You seem visibly affected."

"I think I'm just a little confused. I need to ask some questions. Let's start with: where am I?"

"Miss, You are in my cabin on Knob Creek. I found you on the banks of the Rolling Fork River. I pray I ought find the Doctor if you are unaware of your location."

"Knob Creek, where?"

"Kentucky, Larue County to be precise. Miss, I must insist on escorting you to a physician. You have a severe wound on your head which I fear may be causing you to suffer from some confusion."

"I think you may be right. Before we go, can we talk a little more about where I am and how I got here?"

"Before we converse any further would you grace me with your name?"

"My name is Catherine Beaven." Abe looked startled.

"I will make ready for a trip to the Doctor. I fear you are no longer of sound mind."

"I know I'm confused and I don't know what's happened, but I'm not insane."

As I finished my sentence I began to cry. I was truly frightened. I needed to know what had happened to me and how I could possibly be sitting in Abraham Lincoln's Knob Creek cabin.

The nearest Doctor was in Elizabethtown. Abraham had gone to a neighbor to borrow something suitable for me to wear. He returned with a dress, petticoat, corset and lace up boots. I knew I had somehow ended up in a very rural place but it seemed more and more like I had not just changed geography, I had changed time. I could not understand why I would need to wear a dress, petticoat and corset to see a doctor. While I struggled to dress myself in my new outfit I looked around the cabin. There was no running water, no electricity and no indoor plumbing. I finished dressing and headed outside for the first time since Abraham had brought me to the cabin. As I stepped outside I nearly fainted. Possibly from the corset but most likely from the sight of Abraham and Charlie sitting on a wagon hitched to a team of mules.

"A wagon and mules? That's more than just rural." I said to myself as I climbed on to the wagon seat.

As we drove along the jingle jangle of the trace chains had a hypnotic effect. I stared at the mules feet keeping perfect time with each other as the wagon rocked to and fro, and in my mind I went over and over the events of the day. Both Abraham and I were quiet. He would gaze at me for a moment scratch his head, pull on his beard and go back to focusing on the mules. I went through every detail from the day in my mind trying to establish some facts to work with.

Fact one: I live on a ranch in New Mexico.

Fact two: I work at the National Laboratories in Los Alamos; I have a PhD from Stanford in molecular biology.

Fact Three: I am currently working on the global climate energy project in the area of Biomass energy conversion.

14

Fact Four: Charlie and I spent the night at the lab but I couldn't remember why.

Those were the facts I knew to be true. Next I went over things I remembered and things I could piece together. I remembered a flash and maybe an explosion. I could remember Charlie yelping, his collar smoking, and trying to take it off, when … I couldn't remember what happened after that.

I needed to know what happened to Charlie. I needed to know why Abe had a dog exactly like Charlie. A dog that he too had rescued from a river and subsequently named Charlie. None of this was making any sense. I knew I had hit my head but I certainly didn't hit it that hard.

I was certain, as a scientist I could find some logical explanation. I just needed to look at the evidence and form a hypothesis. Then follow Ockham's Razor, whatever the simplest explanation, no matter how illogical, is most likely true.

Joe Casabona

As I walked into the restaurant I saw Joe stand and smile. The look on his face told me he approved of Chloe's work. I had to admit, although it wasn't an outfit I would have chosen, I did look pretty good and best of all they were my clothes and I felt good in them.

Joe was as stereotypically Northeast as I was Southwest. He had worked for the Lab in the Public Relation Department for twenty years and had overseen every major public announcement for the past decade. It was Joe's job to make science interesting enough to compete in today's media hungry world.

"Damn, you clean up nice Ms. Catherine"

"Thanks Joe, and thanks for sending Chloe, I don't think I scared her to much."

"She's the best and I knew she could handle a wicked old ranch broad like you. Now, sit down and let's go over the plan for today."

"You want to work, before we eat? Joe, are you sick?"

"No, I am just very nervous about this announcement. You didn't give me much time to prepare. You eat, I'll talk and when this is all over we can both drink."

"Sounds like a plan. I'll catch the waiter on his next pass, until then, start talking O' great spin doctor."

"The first thing I'll do is show the presentation you worked up. You did a nice job on that, by the way. If this scientist thing doesn't work out I think you may have a future in marketing. After the presentation I'll have you explain why this technology must be protected and what potential harm could arise from exploiting it. This is where you're going to have to WOW them. It's very important that you don't come across as too much of a science nerd or too condescending."

"Geez Joe, I can't believe you're afraid I might alienate someone."

"Sweetheart, I'm not afraid you'll alienate someone, I'm afraid you will alienate everyone."

"I'll pretend you didn't just call me sweetheart if you find the waiter. A girl could starve to death in this joint."

As Joe and I looked for the waiter I spotted exactly what I didn't want to see. Four big guys, two near the front door and two fast approaching from my left. They had the unmistakable look of security FBI, CIA or some other government acronym. They appeared to be on a mission.

"Shit! Shit! Shit!"

"What's wrong with you?" Joe asked

"Joe, shut up and listen!"

"Hey! What's this about?"

"Look at me Joe, in about five seconds two big leathernecks in black suits are going to escort us out of here. They are coming from my left. Look at me! They have two friends at the front door. Joe, I want you to hit the record button on your iPhone. Put it in your pocket. Just let it record until the battery dies. I had a feeling guys like these would show up. Someone was bound to have a problem with today's announcement and as you know keeping a secret in this town is impossible. I'm about to make a scene. You do exactly as those guys say. Do you hear me Joe? Good luck and don't be a hero. None of this is more important than you."

Before Joe could answer I jumped up and turned over our table right onto his lap. I began screaming profanities and throwing food from the neighboring tables at him. This caused the men in black just enough hesitation for me to make a break for it. I ran right through the kitchen and out into the back alley. I knew these guys were professionals so it was no use to try to outrun them. I needed to outsmart them. I opened every door in the alley as fast as I could then jumped into the dumpster next to the back door and waited. All I could think about was how angry Chloe would be if she knew I was sitting in a heap of trash. I wondered what sort of magic spray she had to remove the stench of garbage.

It didn't take long before there were four men running down the alley checking all the open doors. I waited until I couldn't hear any footsteps and then freed myself from the garbage heap. I quickly doubled back into the kitchen. The kitchen staff started to protest; after all I was covered in garbage and smelled like a skunk. One of them recognized me as friend of Joe's.

Joe was a regular and in true Northeast style had befriended the chef and kitchen staff. Joe was also not shy about showing his gratitude; therefore Joe's presence was always taken note of. Once the staff realized I had been dining with Joe they quickly offered to assist in my escape. They sent me into the wine cellar and then blocked the door behind me. Once inside the wine cellar I thought I would be safe for a while. I needed to calm down and get myself ready. By the time the men in black figured out to look in the wine cellar I would be worlds away.

Hiding in the wine cellar had a few unexpected benefits. There was a bistro table covered in wine glasses and a corkscrew. I went over and chose a very nice bottle of wine, uncorked it and poured myself a glass. As I drank the wine I went over the list of possible people who knew what I was working on and who were determined to stop me. There just weren't that many people who knew and had the resources to hire professionals to come after me. Moreover they seemed to be going to great lengths not to hurt me, just to stop me.

I had warned Joe there were powerful people who, if they knew what I was working on, would like to keep it from becoming public knowledge. Joe had called in some huge favors to have this press conference put together on such short notice. He wanted to make sure my work was judged on its merits but I couldn't let him examine my data until after the press conference. That was something a professional like Joe would've never agreed to if he hadn't have known and respected me for so many years. He understood once we made the announcement it would be like opening Pandora's box. People can't un-know something. I needed to get this information out to benefit humanity but until the press conference it needed to be kept secret to ensure my safety. I really hoped I hadn't put Joe in harms way.

We were standing on the edge of greatness, and it's been my experience that's usually when the ground gives out.

I had calmed down, and although I was still no closer to figuring out who was trying to stop me, I was much closer to evading the men chasing me. I took a few deep breaths and made a few quick calculations.

"It really doesn't matter where I end up, chances are anywhere is safer than here." I told myself as I faded away.

Elizabethtown

Charlie let out one sharp bark, startling me back to the wagon. I lifted my eyes from the mule's feet to the horizon. I could hardly believe what I saw. Off to my right there was a crowd of people circling a wagon. Standing inside the wagon were two young African American women. They were dressed in tattered dresses with rags tied around their heads and they were shackled together at the wrists. The crowd of mostly men was looking at them as if inspecting livestock. As we came along side I could hear the call of the auctioneer. I gasped and started to stand when Abraham gently but forcefully pushed me back into my seat. Before I could utter a word he squared his shoulders and faced me. He voice was calm but stern.

"To exercise your demency upon the unsavory crowd would be noble, unfortunately it would not alter the fate of those young women. However raising the ideas of those pusillanimous men would alter your fate by impairing my ability to offer you adequate protection. Miss, today you must hold your tongue and keep your cogitations private no matter how it vexes you."

I felt tears stream down my cheeks, which were hot with anger, but I said nothing. I knew he was right but the price for my silence was a burning deep inside my soul. I needed to know what had happened to me and where or when I had found myself. As the tears streamed and my head spun I found myself violently ill. Without a word I leapt from the wagon seat and ran behind one of the buildings with Charlie hot on my heels. Abe hitched the wagon and found me crying behind the saloon. I had torn my borrowed dress with my hasty dismount and vomited on my hair. Once more Abe scooped me up like a child and carried me. I buried my head against his chest to hide my shame. I couldn't bear to see any more. I just wanted to go home, my home, to my Charlie. Maybe the doctor could help, maybe I was just very ill and all of this was a just a hallucination or a really bad dream. Somehow I knew I wasn't dreaming and I wasn't hallucinating, but at that moment I really want to be.

Doctor Henry Miller had graduated from the Kentucky School of Medicine as an Allopath in 2003, according to the diploma on the wall. I was very pleased to see he was a real doctor but I was very confused by both the "Kentucky School of Medicine" and "Allopath" neither of which fit with 2003. Everything, Abe's speech pattern, the wagon, the slave auction, seemed to be appropriate for the early 1800's, not the present.

Doctor Miller was a small man, approximately thirty with deep brown eyes and an easy smile. He too, was chewing tobacco and had a significant stain on his chin, which, unlike Abe's was clean-shaven. Without a word he gently began cleaning my face and hair, removing all evidence of my unfortunate illness. He mixed some sodium bicarbonate in a glass and had me drink it to settle my stomach. He then checked my head wound. He never spoke directly to me. He addressed all his questions and findings to Abe. He asked if I had any injuries under my clothing. I was a little shocked at the precision to which Abraham could describe the injuries I had sustained in the river. He claimed to have averted his eyes to protect my modesty but apparently only after taking a complete inventory of my condition. Next Doctor Miller cleaned my head wound with something quite caustic that burned horribly. Without thinking I let out an "Oh Shit!"

This brought the entire process to a sudden and complete halt. Both men stood slack jawed staring at me as though I had just thrown a bucket of cold water on them.

"What?" I demanded. "What's wrong? Are my brains falling out?"

"No Miss, your brains seem to be firmly in your head. It's just your language. I have never heard a proper lady use such vulgarity." Doctor Miller explained.

"Really? You're a doctor and you have never heard a woman say, 'shit'?"

"Miss, if you would please refrain from the use of such offensive language." Doctor Miller rebuked.

Abraham paced in circles pulling on his beard. I had obviously mortified both of these men.

"I'm very sorry for offending the both of you. I think maybe I need to go. Thank you Abraham for saving my life and Doctor Miller, thank you for tending to my injuries. I really do think it is best that I go now."

"No, you mustn't go. Doc, inform her she is required to remain."

"Abraham, there is some wisdom to her decision. Her departure may indeed be the most prudent course of action."

"Miss, if you must take your leave please introduce yourself properly to Doc Miller."

"Abraham, you seem very upset. I will be going now. Thank you again." I turned to leave the office.

"Miss! Your leave has not been granted and will not be until Doc Miller is sensible and complaisant in assisting me in determining your parentage and from whence you came. Until such time you will remain seated and silent!"

I was shocked and a little scared by Abraham's tone.

"Miss, to appease Abraham, would you recite all your memories of the events which brought you to be in Abraham's company?" Doc Miller said calmly.

"Honestly, I am very confused about exactly how I came to be in Abraham's company."

"Miss, what is your name?"

"My name is Catherine Beaven, my father is…"

"Your father is Ben and your mother is Jonna" interrupted Doctor Miller

"How could you possible know that?"

"I am the physician of record for Catherine Beaven, and you will gull me no further. I have had enough of your palavar and have lost all interest in assisting you. I recommend you take your leave immediately!"

"Please, Doctor. Please explain to me how you could possibly know my parents. My mother died when I was a child and not even my close friends know her name. How could you possible know? I promise I am not a charlatan and I am not lying to you."

"Abraham, I demand you remove her from my office at once! I have never lifted a hand in anger against a woman but I am willing to make an exception in the case of someone so willing to deceive."

"Prior to her removal Doc I beg of you one question. Does she or does she not appear to be Catherine Beaven?"

"Abe, Catherine Beaven passed on in this very office last year of the cholera. You are aware of that fact. Ben and Jonna Beaven were unfortunate enough to have four children pass last year. I have had the acquaintance of the Beaven family most of my life and I do rightly believe so have you. What has come over you to accept without cavil the tale of this woman?"

"Doc look at her, look at her eyes," Abe pleaded in a near whisper. I thought I was mistaken or haggard by the grief and my perceptions may have been affected but look at her. I make no claim as to understanding how, but I warrant the woman standing before us is Catherine Beaven, in some form of body or soul. Her hair and the manner of her elocution are different but the timbre of her voice, the tenderness of her sensibility, they remain intact. Doc we are duty bound to aid her, just as the Good Samaritan in The Bible. I must admit to look upon her, harrows up deep feelings of grief. However I do believe allowing harm to come to her would cause us considerable regret. Doc, there exists the possibility that all your efforts to preserve Catherine's life may not have failed entirely."

Doc Miller sat down in his chair opened his desk drawer and pulled out a bottle and two glasses. He poured himself a healthy portion and smaller one for Abe. Abe leaned on the wall and Doc sat in his chair both sipping their whiskey and staring at me.

"Good whiskey," Abe commented.

"Very good, John Hardy barters the monks at Gethsemani for blacksmith work. I accept this as payment for tending to his family."

"One could consider that a fair and equitable trade."

"Our agreement allows only for its use as a medicinal aid. However, today I feel it proper to make an exception."

They were drinking fine Kentucky bourbon made at the Abbey of Gethsemani by Trappist Monks. The craftsmanship that went into making that bottle of bourbon is why there is a federal law that defines and protects bourbon as a solely American product. I could only imagine how wonderful it must taste. I was nearly salivating watching them slowly sip from their glasses. I knew it wouldn't be proper to ask for a taste but I was so very tempted.

Abe spoke breaking my pavlovian fixation.

"Previously I inquired as to your origin and you replied New Mexico."

"Yes, I work at the Los Alamos National Laboratory."

"Could you enlighten us as to the location of 'New' Mexico?" Doc Miller asked.

"Do you have a map?"

"No, I'm a Doctor not a cartographer. I am aware of Mexico but I have never heard mention of New Mexico. Is it part of Mexico?"

"No, but I don't think it matters geographically where I'm from."

"Geographically, how else would one determine location if it weren't with geography?"

"I don't suppose either of you have ever heard the terms: quantum physics, chaos theory, string theory or non-linear particle physics?"

"No" they both said simultaneously.

"I would like to explain to both of you what I know and what life is like where I'm from to see if possibly the three of us can devise a plan for my return. Before I go any further, you must both promise never to disclose what I am about to tell you to another soul. You must also agree that no matter how unbelievable my tale you will not assume I am insane or otherwise not of sound mind."

Dr. Miller and Abraham stepped away and conferred. You could see the distress this was causing them but I felt they were inclined to believe me. Abraham spoke for the two of them.

"We have no reason to question the strength or your character or your honesty. We are however mindful of your current state of injury and conclude you do seem to be suffering some confusion. I myself have been injured and confused and am aware that confusion brought on by injury does not constitute insanity or dishonesty. We vow to assist, to the best of our ability, in your safe and timely return to your family."

"Thank you both. I'll tell you what I do know. Afterward maybe you can help me form a hypothesis. I appear to be someone you both know. Abraham appears to me someone I have read about in history. To my knowledge I know nothing about you Doctor Miller. According to the newspaper lying on the desk, today is approximately five years earlier than it was two days ago for me. From the way people are dressed and behave, today seems to be more in the realm of one hundred and fifty years in my past."

"Are you to say you have journeyed through time?" Abraham questioned.

"I don't think it is that simple."

"You would consider that simple?" Doctor Miller asked.

"No, heavens no, time travel would be anything but simple, what I meant was there seems to be more to what happened than just rewinding time. If I had traveled through time, theoretically it would be like reading a book backwards. The fact that chronological time does not agree with the events of history as I know them is very confusing to me."

"You remarked of reading history books concerning me? Are you quite assured these books were not referencing another? Possibly with the same moniker?"

"I'm positive. You are definitely the Abraham Lincoln I've read about."

"Why would Abraham be someone worthy of mention in history? He is a farmer from Kentucky. I am a Doctor and I bare no illusion of comment in history."

"He is not only a farmer he is a lawyer, right Abe?"

"By what manner did you obtain that information?"

"You will need to use those skills soon. I suggest you work on the rules of debate and parliamentary procedure."

"I was unaware you studied Law."

"I have never told a soul. My studies were in anticipation of marriage. A more suitable occupation for a family man than a farmer I surmised."

"Please take no offense but it appears, women where you are from are much less mannered and delicate. You claim to be a woman of science and you do seem to possess a fair amount of knowledge on that subject. Is that common for a woman or are you an oddity?"

"Seeing that I am not delicate I won't take offense Doc but if your asking if all women are like me then the answer is no."

"Praise be to God."

"What I was going to say Abe is some women hold positions of power and esteem much higher than mine. It is not uncommon to see a woman in any given profession. We have proven our ability to maintain careers and families simultaneously."

"Was I amiss in my assumption that you are an unwed woman?"

"No, your assumption is correct Doc. I have never married but out of choice not lack of opportunity."

"This opportunity you refer to, will he be grieved by your disappearance?"

"Yes Abraham, I'm afraid both he and my father will be suffering tremendously by now. I need to find my way back to them as soon as possible."

"Then allow me to ask you again. Please recite all of your memories from the day Abraham found you by the river."

I did my very best to tell Doc and Abraham everything I remembered. We talked for several hours going over every detail. A theory of what had happened began to develop but there were still so many unanswered questions. Finding explanations for the time discrepancies, the shift in locations and Charlie would take more than one evening to solve but I was feeling a little less frightened and a little more optimistic about returning home.

"Gentlemen, my head is hurting and I don't think we are going to solve this problem tonight. It is a long wagon ride back to the cabin. I think Abraham and I should be on our way."

"It is ill advised for you to commence any further travel. The wound on your head is deep and I believe there may exist some swelling in your cranium. I will inform Ms. O'Bryan in the boarding house to ready a room for your use. Abe will escort you once all arrangements have been completed. I will give you a tonic to take with water before bed to aid with your sleep."

"Thank you Doc."

"We will continue our discussion in the morning. I do regret raising my voice and requesting your removal. Your circumstance is quite vexing but that is a poor excuse for my uncouthed behavior."

"No need to apologize Doc."

"Abe, please escort her in through the kitchen in approximately ten minutes. There is no need to raise the alarm of another soul in town."

The Land of Enchantment

They call New Mexico the land of enchantment and it's easy to see why in the fall. October has always been my favorite month on the ranch. The days are long and warm but the nights are cold and crisp. Everything seems to be soaking up as much sun and color as possible before winter sets in. The soft evening light against the golden leaves of the cottonwoods transforms the bosque into a shimmering golden paradise. More often than not I enjoy these last rays of golden sunshine aboard one of my trusty ranch horses.

My ranch is bordered by the Rio Grande on the West, which allows for easy access to the bosque. I sneak in a sunset ride after work whenever possible. Most of these rides are quite peaceful and uneventful but occasionally I come across some feral cattle, the odd black bear or even our resident mountain lion. This night however, none of the usual suspects interrupted my solitude, it was the crying of a puppy that caught my attention. At first I thought it was a coyote trying to trick me. They are famous for calling in unsuspecting critters and then ganging up on them, but a human on horseback is a tall order for a coyote. I followed the yips and yaps to the riverbank. Up and down the riverbank I rode, unable to find the source of the frantic sound until I finally dismounted and hung my head over the edge. Sure enough the bank was cutaway and stuck against it was the cutest little black and silver speckled pup you've ever seen. He had two black ears, a speckled muzzle and silver eyelashes. When he closed his eyes they just disappeared into his spots. He was shivering from the cold and chin deep in water with no way out. I grabbed my rope and gently tried to rope him under his front legs. He didn't have much fight left, so I managed to get the rope around him without too much trouble. I dallied the other end to "Gunny" my gunmetal grey roan and gave him the cue to start backing real slow. Gunny was a good ranch horse, and he knew we had a wee one on the end of that rope. He just eased back nice and slow making sure to keep tension on the rope so as not to drop the pup but not pulling hard enough to hurt him. I lay on my belly and guided the rope away from the bank. In no time Gunny and I had ourselves a pup.

I unzipped my barn coat and stuck the poor wet and shivering puppy up close to my chest. I zipped him in, climbed back into the saddle and headed for the barn. It was dark by the time we made it back, and my new little friend was sound asleep inside my coat. I took my coat off and laid it, with the dog in it, on the haystack while I did my chores. By the time the horses were fed and I was ready to go to the house I was freezing and the pup was warm and dry. I carried him into the house and started a fire, then dug through the fridge and found some eggs and hamburger meat. I figured that would make a dinner we could both eat. After we shared our first meal together I decided I should give him a name.

"What should I call you little fella? How about Lucky? You're definitely lucky. Maybe Fido, I've never actually known a dog named Fido. Maybe Charlie, you look as sorry as the Charlie Brown Christmas Tree."

With that, the pup got up, crawled into my lap and gave me a big kiss on the end of my nose.

"So Charlie it is. Let's make you a bed, it looks like you're here to stay."

The next morning Charlie was rearing to go to the barn.

"All right, all right, let me get my coffee and we'll go feed. Then you are going to have to stay in the laundry room until I get back from work. Sorry, but until I get you a kennel that will have to do."

Out the door and to the barn little Charlie ran, coming back to check on me every few minutes. He stayed right by my side until I had completed my chores. Then, just as I was headed to the house, off he ran, right toward the river.

"You've got to be kidding me. Charlie didn't you learn anything from your last trip to the river?"

I grabbed a halter and a lead rope and hopped up on Roxy, a sweet little palomino mare. With a swift kick I asked her to take me to the river. She protested a bit about leaving her breakfast but since she was a good horse she complied. I couldn't catch Charlie even at gallop until we reached the river. When I finally caught him he was sitting on the bank right beside the spot where I had fished him out of the river. I hopped off Roxy and tried to grab him. That's when he started barking at me.

"What is wrong with you Charlie? I've got to get to work and I don't want to play. Now come here so I can get back to the house!"

I reached out again but he stayed just out of reach. He kept circling back to the riverbank while looking down and barking.

"Okay, what are you trying to tell me, Charlie?"

Once again I lay down and hung my head over the edge of the riverbank.

"Holy cow Charlie, how did I miss that last night? Damn it I didn't bring a rope, and I don't know if I can reach it."

Charlie brought me to the river to find his collar. It was no ordinary collar. It was made of red leather and it had a large green gemstone in the center, which was flanked, by two smaller gemstones on either side. I couldn't tell exactly what kind, but it was definitely a very expensive collar, which meant Charlie probably had a nice home to go back to. I looked around and found a stick with a forked end. I managed to hook the collar on the stick. With another stick I managed to work the collar up within reach. The entire time Charlie was jumping in circles in the middle of my back.

"Ya know Charlie this might be easier if you weren't using me as a trampoline."

Finally I managed to get the collar within reach and grabbed it. As I rolled onto my back, I was besieged with Charlie kisses.

"I don't think I've ever met a dog so happy to get his collar back. Okay hold still and I'll put it on you. Hey, just a second! There is an inscription on the back. Maybe it's your name or the name of your owner."

I took off my wild rag and wiped the collar clean. I read the inscription. Then I read it several more times before I was sure I had read it right. The inscription read:

"Charlie"

If found please call

Catherine Beaven @ LANL

I couldn't figure out what kind of joke this was? Had someone almost drowned a puppy in order to play a practical joke? I strapped the collar around Charlie's neck, stuffed him back inside my barn coat, swung up on Roxy and headed for the barn. I was cold, wet, confused and late for work. As soon as I got back to the barn I turned Roxy out and ran to the house, where I started the shower and made a quick call to work.

"Hey Kevin, I'm running a little late, don't start the experiment without me. Thanks see ya in about an hour."

As I ran into the bathroom, Charlie parked himself right in the doorway. I started to protest but I really didn't have the time.

"Fine, just stay put, don't tear up anything and for Christ's sake don't pee on the floor."

After a quick pass through the shower, I dried, applied my lotion and was ready to get dressed when Charlie snuck up and gave my leg a quick lick.

"Hey that tickles! You're quite the little troublemaker aren't you? I have to go, so off to the laundry room with you."

Like a good soldier Charlie marched off to the laundry room and snuggled up in his new bed.

"Well, you seem comfy. I'll be back as soon as I can, until then no barking, no chewing and no peeing on the floor."

As I drove up the canyon to the lab, gulping down my third cup of coffee, I went over the morning's events in my head again.

Charlie is a puppy, maybe ten-twelve weeks old; he seems very smart and very attached to his collar. He appears healthy, well fed and has a collar, so probably not a stray. Which begs the question: how did he end up in the river? If someone was messing with me and dumped him at the ranch, they wouldn't have left him by the river, it's half mile from the gate and surely he wouldn't have gone down there by himself. Although as evidence by his performance this morning he is perfectly capable of getting down there. So how and why did a puppy end up in the Rio Grande with a very expensive collar inscribed with my name and his name that I just gave him last night? None of this makes any sense.

I was still carrying on quite the conversation with myself as I parked my car and walked toward the lab.

"Catherine, you all right?" A familiar voice rang out from the front door of our lab.

"I'm fine Kevin, just a little rattled but what else is new? Do you have everything ready for our experiment?"

"Yes Ma'am, all the data is entered and triple checked. We only need the Queen herself to give her blessing so we can see if we have created a new energy source."

"The Queen, huh? That's not what you labbies call me behind my back now is it?"

"Why of course it isn't. We would never disrespect anyone with your standing," Kevin rebutted with a wink.

"Just as I suspect, you'll say anything to protect your spot on this project." I retorted with proper sarcasm.

As we walked into the building, I left the morning's troubles behind and focused on the work at hand. We'd been working for

36

months to set this experiment up and if it worked as we hoped, we were well on our way to efficiently converting cheap renewable biological material into a sustainable source of energy, the by product of which is desalinated seawater, effectively ending our dependence on fossil fuel while also providing clean drinking water. Our society could finally move past the industrial age and into the next era of human evolution.

Because of the potential harm this new technology posed to some of the world's most powerful corporate giants, our project was classified as top secret. Our lab was in a nondescript concrete building tucked in a complex of nondescript concrete buildings at Los Alamos National Labs (LANL). Inside the lobby were two armed military guards who stood like sentries guarding the biometric scanners required to gain access. Every day for the past four years I had spoken to them, and every day for the past four years they stared back and me and politely pointed to the retina scanner and palm readers mounted on the wall. As Kevin and I crossed the lobby, once again I glibly recited:

"Good morning gentlemen, thanks for being here again this morning, have a nice day."

To my and Kevin's shock, the guard on the left replied,

"Good Morning Catherine." Then he winked and stared straight ahead.

I wasn't sure what to do so I just completed my bio-scans and stepped into the elevator.

"Wow! I thought they must be mute!" Kevin exclaimed as soon as the elevator doors closed.

"I can't believe that after four years one of them decides to get a little cheeky. There must be something in the air today.

Maybe Mars is in retrograde or some crap like that. After this experiment runs today I swear I'll have something tall and dark waiting for me at home."

"Oh my, you have a date tonight?"

"No, you moron, I have a six pack of Guinness in the fridge. I swear you kids need to get out of this lab and off your computers more often."

"Forgive me for saying so ma'am but since joining this project there hasn't exactly been a lot time for anything other than the lab and computers."

"Fair enough, so promise when this project is done you will take some time to live a little."

"Maybe I'll come to your ranch and let you teach me to ride a horse. How's that?"

"Well, that's a start. Anyway, let's get to work. The sooner we finish, the sooner you can get out of here."

My entire team, along with a few V.I.P.'s from the LANL had assembled in the lab for our experiment. The reality was most of the experiment had been under way for months. This wasn't some Hollywood set with lots of glass tubes and flashing lights on computer consoles. It was very anti-climactic real science. Twenty plus people were going to be standing around watching a light bulb and a water glass. If the light bulb lit and the water that dripped into the glass was clean potable water our system worked on a very small scale. If our microclimate was set correctly to decompose the biomaterial it would create the energy needed to light the light bulb and the waste product would be clean water. After one last check of the data I was satisfied.

"Okay then, I guess I should make some sort of speech about how the acquisition of technology moves all civilizations forward but really, just turn the damn thing on and let's see what happens."

That received a hearty cheer from my staff and some frowns from our esteemed guests. Within moments the light bulb began to flicker evening out to a steady glow.

"Fantastic we're batting 500 already. Come on baby make us some water." I begged

Everyone was holding their breath and staring at the water glass. It was like the old ketchup ad. Anticipation. Then with a sound heard around the lab the first drop fell into the glass. The entire lab exhaled.

"Now, someone test the sample and let me know what's in that water."

Kevin was already on it.

"Just a few more seconds ma'am and I'll know for sure. It's pure water. No salt, no impurities. It's cleaner than the bottled water in the fridge."

"Shut it down. Evacuate the environment so we can set it up again. You know the rule, it's only valid if we can repeat it. Great work everyone, great work. Drinks are on me, 8pm El Paragua."

While my staff dealt with the project I dealt with the politicking, my least favorite part of my job. I was doing my very best glad-handing when I received an urgent call.

"So sorry gentlemen. I have to take this. "I'll be sure to answer all your questions in my report." I reassured them as I headed for my office.

"Hey Dad what's up? Are you okay? You used the 999 so what's the emergency?"

"Jorge called me this morning after you left and said the Drafts had gotten out again and he could use some help. I headed over to the ranch to give him a hand. When I got there your gate was open, which seemed very odd, so I went straight to the house. The door was open and there was a black speckled pup sitting on you sofa. Other than that nothing seemed out of place. When did you get a dog anyway? No matter, I have the dog with me, the drafts are back in and the gate is locked. Jorge said he didn't see anyone come through the gate, but he was in the shop welding when I got there, so he would have missed the second coming of Christ. Should I be worried about this or were you just a cup of coffee low when you left this morning?"

"I was definitely short on caffeine, but I know the door was closed and so was the gate. I'll have one of the guys from work check it out before I go home. Thanks for taking the dog. His name is Charlie. I felt bad leaving him this morning. I'll explain everything later. I wont be home 'til late tonight, but tomorrow should be a short day. Do you want to have dinner at the ranch?"

"Sure I'll watch your new little friend until tomorrow but you know it's gonna cost ya. Oh and one other thing, did you set your iPod to play only "Cake"?"

"I offered dinner and heavens no, you know I leave it on 'shuffle'. It was playing Jerry Jeff when I left."

"Oh well, you better check that when you get home and I think this will cost dinner and dessert."

"Fine I'll make sure to pick up the Ben & Jerry's on my way home. Thanks again Dad, and try not to ruin the dog before I get back. Love ya."

"Love you too kid be careful."

Most of the bigwigs had filtered back to their respective holes, but the military liaison was still chatting Kevin up. I really didn't like the military knowing anything about this project but I did understand that when you work at a government funded lab the military has its fingers in everything. The up side to having the ever-present military was there was also an ever-present security presence.

"Major Allen, may I have a word with you?" I requested in my most professional voice.

"Yes Ma'am, how can I be of assistance?"

"I have reason to believe someone committed or tried to commit a black bag job on my home this morning. Could you please send some of your investigators over there and check for any prints on my iPod, laundry room door, office door and pay special attention to my desk drawer. My prints should be the only prints you find on the desk or any of the drawers."

"Ma'am you know if I do that you will have to report a breach in security"

"Major, how will I know if there has been a breach until you have checked? If you find something I will follow the proper protocol. If your highly skilled and trained military agents tell me no one has been in my house, I can skip the mountain of paperwork that I really don't have time for. I'm not asking you to run and unauthorized op just check it out and make sure I was just having a real bad morning."

"Okay but if there is so much as a whiff of a security breech this goes right to my superiors."

"Thank you Major Allen, I'm sure it's nothing but I'm just a little edgy right now. I'm sure a bottle of the Taos Lighting you're so fond of will find it's way to you soon."

"That won't be necessary Ma'am. If you are in any danger it is my honor to protect you."

"Major Allen if I didn't know better I would swear you just made a pass at me."

"Did it work?"

"Maybe, you know I never throw myself at a man I don't think is a good catch."

"Ma'am I will have my men check on things and get back to you, say around twenty three hundred hour at the ranch?"

"That should be just fine Major."

I always forget what lushes labbies can be when they are celebrating. I thought I would be able to buy a couple of rounds at the local watering hole and be back to the ranch long before ten. Instead it was ten before I was finally able to settle my tab and drag myself away from some very grateful yet very inebriated lab techs. The Major was supposed to be at the ranch in about an hour, and I still had a couple of reports to finish about todays experiment. Thank God Jorge had taken care of the horses and Dad had Charlie if not there would be no hope of anything other than work tonight. I knew If I hurried I could send some lame email about the experiment results taking more time to calculate, catch a quick shower and have a drink ready for the Major before he arrived. I pressed a little harder on the accelerator trying to expedite my trip home. As I turned off the highway, I saw the blue light come on.

"Shit, Damn, Piss and all the other profanities! Come on not tonight, I just want to go home. I haven't had a quiet night at home with the Major for weeks." I was in full whine by the time the officer got to my window.

"Evening Ma'am, I'm officer Martinez. Do you know why I pulled you over?"

"Honestly officer Martinez, No, but I'm sure you will be happy to inform me."

"Ma'am, have you been drinking this evening?"

"Is that why you pulled me over? To ask if I had been drinking?"

"Ma'am would you please step out of the vehicle."

"I'm guessing that's not really a request, is it officer Martinez?"

"No Ma'am it's not. Step out of the vehicle."

"With pleasure officer, anything else I can do for you this lovely evening?"

"Ma'am if you continue to be difficult, I will have to detain you."

"Difficult? Oh buddy you haven't seen difficult yet, but I'm sure I can work myself into it."

"Ma'am would you please turn around and put you hands on your head."

"No, no sir I will not. I haven't done anything wrong, you haven't informed me why I was stopped and you certainly have no reason to arrest me. You better either ticket me now, let me go, or call for back up!"

As I finished that sentence I realized that I had probably just crossed a line that was going to involve some sort of penalty and I was right. Before I could utter a "sorry, just kidding," Officer Martinez had me pinned against the car and was handcuffing me. I thought about apologizing or protesting but I decided I had already said too much, and silence was probably my best friend at that point. Just as I was being placed in the back seat of Officer Martinez's squad car I saw Major Allen drive by, then stop and come back.

"Great I will never hear the end of this." I mumbled to myself.

Major Allen was talking to Officer Martinez, no doubt explaining that he would take full responsibility for me and that something like this would never happen again. I wasn't sure how I felt about the good ole' boy thing going on, but if it got me home any sooner I wasn't going to fight it. Major Allen came to the squad car first.

"Hey, there how's it going?" He started with a heavy dose of sarcasm.

"Not great, but could be worse."

"The nice officer said he is charging you with drunk and disorderly, DUI, speeding, assaulting an officer and anything else he thinks might stick. You really charmed him, didn't ya?"

"First off I am not drunk, so there goes the D&D and DUI, I haven't admitted to speeding, and hurting his feelings hardly constitutes assaulting and officer."

"I see you have been practicing your contrition."

"Fine, I'm so sorry, it will never happen again. Now please let me blow into his little machine so we can get to the ranch for a quiet evening alone."

"I'll tell him you have agreed to a sobriety test and expressed deep remorse. Hopefully that will soothe the very riled Officer Martinez. Now before you do anything else silly, you will pass the breathalyzer won't you?"

"Yes! I nursed one margarita with dinner for over two and a half hours. The evening wouldn't have been as painfully long if I had drank more and you know I don't drink and drive."

"I know and that's what I told your new friend. Now let's go play nice and maybe we can still salvage the evening."

I passed my breathalyzer with flying colors and Officer Martinez sent me home without so much as a traffic ticket. I did promise to donate to the policemen's ball and try to be kinder to all of the cities finest. Major Allen and I were safe on the ranch in no time.

"I can't believe you offered to donate to the policemen's ball. You're lucky he doesn't know that joke or I would be bailing your ass out of jail right now," the Major started while I mixed us some drinks.

"For what, inappropriate timing of a joke? I hadn't done anything wrong and I still don't know why he pulled me over in the first place."

"Were you speeding?"

"Yeah before I turned off the highway, but he was parked on the shoulder after the turn and I hadn't had a chance to even get up to the speed limit, so I certainly hadn't broken it yet. I don't think this is the Minority Report, so I should've been innocent for at least another quarter of a mile. What did he tell you?

"Actually he didn't say why he initially pulled you over, just that you were drunk and very belligerent. I believed the belligerent part but I knew you wouldn't be driving drunk. Can we just forget about Officer Martinez and enjoy some good bourbon, some good music and a quiet evening together?"

"The iPod is plugged in. Just turn up the volume on the stereo, sit down beside me on the couch and we can talk about the first thing that pops up."

"You think you are real cute don't you?"

"Well, aren't I?

The Forbidden City

"Damn! Damn, damn it! I missed it by a mile."

I knew immediately I hadn't been entirely focused, which wasn't a huge surprise considering the circumstances, but it certainly complicated my life. Particularly since that "mile" I missed it by was a vertical mile not a horizontal mile.

At least I have a commanding view. However, I'm going to freeze to death. Somehow this doesn't seem any better than dealing with the goons in the restaurant. Okay, just relax you know the drill. Chances are someone will come along shortly, that's how it works. Granted this is the first time I have ended up on top of a mountain but have a little faith Catherine, you'll see everything is going to be just fine.

With my little pep talk completed I began evaluating my situation. The good news was I had on my boots; the bad news was I had on a chiffon blouse. The good news, I arrived unharmed, bad news I would be dead in a matter of hours if I did not find some shelter from the wind and make a fire. Good news, it was still daylight, bad news, not for long. With that realization I started looking for a trail or path, something I could follow. I was about 1,000 feet above the tree line. I couldn't find any definite path through the snow and rocks but I could see what appeared to be a trail at the edge of the trees. As long as I stayed upright and avoided a nasty fall I should be able to make it to the trail where I could get out of the howling wind.

I headed down the mountain with a slow and tentative pace. I managed to get myself safely to the trees before the sun went down. I gathered as much wood as I could haul and found a fallen tree to block the wind. There were plenty of pine boughs that had been blown down, so I was able to fashion myself a rather nice and soft lean-to structure without too much effort. Finally, I reached in my skirt pocket and pulled out the two things I ALWAYS have: a lighter and some chap stick. Having spent most of my life living at altitude, I am painfully aware of how fast the weather can change and how quickly a situation can go from bad to deadly if you can't start a fire. Unfortunately I was not born with the fire starter gene. I am woefully incompetent when it comes to making a fire, so for self-preservation and a hundred and one other uses, I always have a lighter. The chap stick is also a necessity in a mountainous climate, and it doubles as wax to help start a fire. I made a nice little nest of dry pine needles, put a glob of chap stick right in the middle, broke some small twigs and formed a tepee. Then with the power of the almighty Bic lighter, I lit my little teepee. Voila, fire. In no time at all I was nestled down in my pine bough bed with a nice fire to keep me warm.

"If this works like I think… Charlie should be here soon. I guess this is what happens when you aren't calm and focused. Measure twice cut once, Catherine," I chided to myself.

I had nearly resigned myself to spending the night on the mountainside alone when I heard Charlie.

"Charlie, come here you crazy dog. Boy am I happy to see you. Who have you hooked up with now? Someone special I bet, no matter, I'm sure I will like them, you always have great taste in people."

I could hear a male voice calling for Charlie. He had an accent maybe German, maybe Russian. It was hard to tell from here but the good news was I had found Charlie yet again. Everything else would work it self out just like always. It wasn't long before the gentleman found us. He was a handsome man in his early twenties, quite fit with blonde hair and blue eyes. He seemed very at home in the mountains. He spoke German or possibly Austrian, I've never been very good with my Germanic languages but whatever it was he was speaking I couldn't understand him. He seemed quite impressed with both my shelter and my clothing. The one word I could pick out was "gypsy" or something along those lines. Chloe had done such a "fabulous" styling job that I was being mistaken for a gypsy. I suddenly felt a little self-conscience. I tried to introduce myself and with a lot of pointing and sign language we managed to communicate our names.

His name was Peter Aufschnaiter. He was some sort of alpinist and it became clear he felt it was too late to begin a trek down the mountain. We would have to spend the night in my little shelter. Peter had been prepared for an overnight stay on the mountain. He had a small rucksack with some hard cheese, canned sardines, some amazing dark bread, an extra pair of socks and best of all a fine woolen sweater. Peter graciously offered the sweater and socks to help keep me warm. I quickly accepted his hospitality and donned my new attire. Peter divided up the bread; cheese and sardines then went out and gathered a tremendous armload of wood. With our bellies full and enough wood to get us through the night Peter, Charlie, and I were ready to turn in. I placed my back against the log, then Charlie snuggled in close, Peter was left more exposed but closest to the fire. We were cozy and warm and within moments we were all fast asleep.

Peter kept the fire going all night while Charlie and I slept. As soon as my eyes opened, Charlie gave me a couple of good licks and went off for his morning walk about. Peter was up and nearly ready to go before I managed to crawl out of my nest.

"Good Morning Peter, don't suppose you have any coffee hidden in that bag of yours?" Peter smiled and chuckled a little.

"Cooffeee" I emulated, mimicking drinking from a cup.

"Nien"

"That's kind of what I suspected. How about we get off this mountain and see what your world has to offer in the way caffeine and protein."

Peter smiled politely not understanding a word I had just spoken. As we headed off the mountain he gave a quick whistle for Charlie and began to hum Edelweiss. It wasn't long until Charlie caught up, sticking his nose under my skirt and giving my leg a quick lick.

"Really! Every morning? I didn't even put lotion on; why do you do that?"

After about an hour we had made our way around to the opposite side of the mountain from our camp. The trees thinned and we emerged into a massive high mountain valley. The view was breathtaking. I paused for a moment just soaking in the majesty. I've spent most my life in the mountains and I've seen a lot of alpine meadows and valleys, this was one of the most spectacular sights I had ever glimpsed. I had assumed I must be somewhere in Europe considering Peter, but these were not

50

European mountains. There aren't any mountains in Europe this tall or this rugged.

"Where on earth have I ended up this time Charlie?" Charlie just gave me a head tilt and headed off in the direction of a small village I could barely make out in the distance. The sun was warm on my back but the air was fresh and crisp. I was very grateful for the sweater and the socks even at mid-day. The aspen trees were at the height of their golden color and if you listened closely their leaves sounded like thousands of tiny bells ringing in the breeze. The valley was still verdant and green but I could tell these were the waning days of fall. Winter would arrive soon and I would have to guess winter in this valley was long and very, very hard. As we approached the village I noticed prayer flags flapping in the breeze around the small huts.

"So this isn't Kansas Toto." I mumbled.

Peter turned to see if I was trying to communicate with him. I waved him off and just smiled. My mind had started spinning, Peter Aufschnaiter, Buddhist prayer flags, huge mountains.

Come on Catherine, come on, put it all together, German in the Himalayan or possibly the Ural mountains, Buddhists, winter closing in, why would this be important? Why here, why now? You can figure this out. Just follow Charlie's lead and you'll be back in no time.

My internal dialogue had distracted me from the fact we had arrived at the door of a small, thatch-roofed hut. Peter knocked twice then walked in. I followed ducking down to get through the doorway. Once inside, the hut was quite spacious. From the inside I could see the hut was completely round. The roof timbers were pitched upward to provide ample headroom. There was a coal burning stove sitting precisely in the middle of the room. The stovepipe went through a hole in the roof naturally formed by the way the timbers had been set. The floor was wooden, and the walls were made of a very heavy canvas lined with animal hides. There were piles of pillows covered in colorful and ornate silk fabrics stacked at even intervals along the walls. A few cupboards and low tables were scattered throughout the single room but no chairs. As my eyes adjusted to the dim lighting, I spotted a figure lying on some pillows toward the far wall. They were almost completely covered by a pile of fur blankets with only a pair of boots sticking out one end and a shock of blonde hair at the other.

"Heinrich, Heinrich" Peter shouted

"Stop schreien. Was wilst du?" Heinrich mumbled from under the pile of blankets.

"Sei und Englisch Frau gast. Aufstehen!" Peter commanded

When Heinrich heard the word "Englisch Frau" he bolted upright.

"Guten, I mean good day, Miss." Heinrich began as he tried to find his bearings and make himself presentable.

"Wonderful, you speak English. I'm so relieved."

"Yes, I speak English and so can Peter but after our detainment by the British he refuses to."

"You sot! You let me mumble on and on to myself the whole time understanding every word. How dare you." I fired of to Peter.

Heinrich found my fury quite amusing.

"Ya, once again Peter you have impressed a lady. How could it be you have no wife?" Heinrich jabbed at Peter who was looking rather sheepish.

"I'm sorry for my friend's unforgivable behavior, he has forgotten what few manners he once knew. Please allow me introduce myself. I am Heinrich Harrer," he began.

"Peter and I traveled a very long distance with much difficulty to find ourselves in this foreign land. We have not had the pleasure of any Anglo company for quite some time. Please forgive me but I can not help but wonder how is it you could have ended up in Lhasa?"

This was awkward. How was I to explain I'd literally just appeared on the side of a mountain? I had no idea what to tell them that didn't sound like complete lunacy, even to me. I slowly began my explanation. I hoped they wouldn't haul me off to an insane asylum. I did find some comfort in the thought there probably weren't any asylums near by and, Heinrich and Peter seemed like fairly educated, intelligent and reasonable men. Even if they didn't understand I didn't think they would let any harm come to me. I really needed to get back to my press conference and more importantly figure who was leaking information at my lab.

Clarissy Savoree

The sun was making its way through the slit in the drapes onto my pillow. I rolled over hoping to sleep a little longer and caught the unmistakable smell of buttermilk biscuits, bacon, eggs and sausage gravy. My eyes slowly opened and I thought to myself if there is a God in the heavens there will be coffee to go along with that magnificent breakfast someone is cooking.

As my vision sharpened I looked around my room. It was beautifully appointed with what I would consider antiques, but it would seem they were relatively new. I was still trying to get my mind around where I was and what had happened. Yesterday after the initial shock had subsided both Abe and Doc Miller were quite helpful in sorting out the details of my current situation. From the consensus of our group, I was indeed Catherine Beaven. I was not the Catherine Beaven that either of the men had known. I physically looked like the Catherine Beaven they had known, but according to Abraham I was slightly older and according to Doc Miller I had better teeth. There also appeared to be genetic similarities between myself the other Catherine. We were both left handed, had green eyes and both were red heads as children whose hair had darkened to an auburn brown. What I needed to understand was, if the Catherine Beaven who had died a year ago and I were the same person genetically, what if anything did that have to do with how I ended up here? More importantly, what affect would that have on my ability to leave? Those were just the questions that needed to be answered, but only after some breakfast.

I drug myself out of the very soft bed, dressed again in my draconian corset and petticoat then headed down the stairs of the boarding house to find the source of that amazing smell. There was a jovially round woman at the bottom of the stairs who greeted me with a very Irish good morning.

"Good morning Mrs. O'Bryan. Thank you again for your hospitality. Abraham and I had not planned on spending the night in town, but Doctor Miller did not think I needed to travel the long distance back to the cabin"

"Yes, of course dear, I'm quite sure you and Abraham had substantial cause for the late hour of your arrival."

Some things never change. Busy body innkeepers always have a way of making one feel bad for things they haven't done.

I was pleased to see Abraham and Doc Miller sharing a table for breakfast.

"Do you mind if I join you gentlemen?" I asked politely.

"I'm not at all certain it would be proper. Please take a seat at the table by the window. After the Doctor and I are sated will resume our conversations his office." Abraham instructed in an all too dismissing tone.

"Fine! I'll enjoy my breakfast in peace and without the unpleasant influence of either of you characters," I retorted in an equally dismissive tone.

Doc Miller couldn't contain his chuckle as I walked to my table.

"She has a sharp wit and gives out very little sugar. I felt your path was difficult before, however, I do believe this Catherine may be more vexing."

"May we eat our breakfast without further personal chaffing? Let us find a way to return that woman back from whence she came."

Abe pleaded between clenched teeth.

"Calm yourself. I was not making you out to be foolish. I only ask that you consider 'that woman' was once held your highest affection. You have spent the past year hobbled by the grief of her loss. Although she is not the same Catherine 'that woman' is very nearly the same. Maybe your spirit could be lifted by her company if you tempered your ire."

"Do you think me to be so dull that I have not considered the benefit of accepting her? I do imagine my spirit would indeed be lifted if I could muster some emotion toward her. The day I discovered her nearly drown, in miserable condition looking in a far worse state than Charlie did the day I plucked him from the same river, I carried her back to my cabin and sat in a chair the night through watching her sleep. I will admit to you and not another soul, I wept. I have mourned Catherine's passing and now it is as though that wound has been reopened and salt has been poured inside. Everything is raw and painful and my very soul burns at the sight of her. I beg of you Doc, as my friend, please aid in the quest to return her, so I can bury my Catherine and mourn no more."

I had walked over to the table where Abe and Doc Miller were sitting to ask about the payment for my room and board. I was standing just behind Abe's right shoulder and heard his admissions to Doc. Doc had seen me standing there but didn't warn Abe. I think he knew we both needed to hear what Abe had to say. As I stood motionless listening, tears began to stream down my cheeks. I couldn't begin to imagine the pain my presence was causing this kind and gentle man. I had been enthralled by the happenstance meeting of Abraham Lincoln. Out of pure selfishness I had been trying to discern whether this Abe Lincoln would have the same impact as the one I was so familiar with. It had never occurred to me that I had somehow played such an important role in his life. That wasn't written in any history book, but then again, this wasn't history. Somehow this was the present. I turned to walk away hoping that Abe would never know I had been eavesdropping. Unfortunately I still hadn't mastered the skirt and petticoat so as I turned, my skirt swung into Abe's table, knocking his coffee cup into his lap. I was so mortified that I just ran out of the room, out of the inn and right into the middle of the street where I was nearly run over by a carriage. The driver of the carriage seemed as startled by our encounter as I was. I tried to apologize but found myself running further down the street with Charlie at my side. Once I began to run it was like my feet had a mind all their own and I had no power to stop them. I ran out of town across a tobacco field and to a small creek. I was about to make my best attempt at jumping across, when I heard a young woman say.

"Miss, I would hate to see you ruin that fine dress or worse yet drown yourself by such a foolhardy act."

I stopped for the first time since spilling Abe's coffee and looked around. I had run quite a distance and everything seemed quieter and more still there by the creek. The young woman who had broken the spell of my runaway feet was squatting at the edge of the creek doing what appeared to be her laundry. She was a lovely young woman with skin the color of a perfectly made latte. Her hair was dark but straight without a hint of a curl. She appeared poor but not destitute. She was wearing a beautiful calico print skirt with a white blouse that was starched to… well it could have held her upright. Both were old and slightly worn but she presented them in the best possible light. She had removed her shoes and socks, they were sitting in the grass behind her, and tucked her skirt up to keep it from getting wet while she beat a basket of clothes over some carefully arranged rocks.

"You're right, of course you are, and worst of all this dress is borrowed. Ruining it would cause quite a stir." I said as I tried to gather myself and wipe the tearstains from my cheeks.

"Miss, It appears as though you have already done that lovely dress some considerable harm. If you will remove it from your person, I have needle and thread at hand. In a short time I can mend and clean the tobacco resin off. Nary a soul should be around so your modesty will suffer not harm. Your petticoat will keep you from catching a chill. I will have you cleaned and presentable and no one will have to know about your episode."

Before I could formulate an answer the young woman was unbuttoning my dress and lifting it over my head.

"Mercy Miss, who aided with your dress this morning?" The girl asked.

"Aided with my dress? Why, no one. I've been dressing myself for quite sometime now."

"I beg your pardon Miss I only meant to ask why your corset is on upside down and back to front. I can right that situation if you would please you?"

I was humiliated. I am an educated woman along with being pretty darn handy. I can fix a computer and a fence; I have a PhD for Christ's sake. How could I not be able to put on a damn dress! I paced in circles berating myself while the young woman began repairing my dress. I had forgotten about the rip I had made when I jumped off the wagon. Apparently my jaunt through the tobacco field had increased the rip in size.

I had not realized it as I was running, but tobacco leaves are coated with a sticky resin and I was covered in it. I sat in the grass and removed my boots and socks, hiked up my petticoat then waded into the creek to try to wash up a bit. The water was cool and refreshing but didn't budge the tobacco resin.

"You will need soap to remove the tobacco. Look in the basket." The young woman instructed.

"Thank you. By the way, what is your name?" I asked as I washed.

"Clarissy, Clarissy Savoree. Now mind you don't rub yourself raw with that soap. I made it with extra lye for the laundry. Once you are clean come on up here and allow me to right your corset. I can't bear the thought of how uncomfortable it must be."

"Clarissy you are too kind. Honestly I just thought they were designed to be uncomfortable."

"Well, Miss, I suppose they are, but no need in making them any worse. They do give you a right nice figure, not that you need any help in that area. You seem to be built nice and sturdy with good hips for child bearing and a right thin waist, if I may be bold enough to say."

"It would appear you are quite bold enough, Clarissy. I think I am somewhat clean so would you please help me with this corset."

"You didn't put your under shirt on this morning Miss." Clarissy chastised.

"Long story but I don't have one."

"Take one of mine from over yonder drying on the bank. Without an undershirt this corset will rub you something fierce."

"So I noticed, I already have sores in some very sensitive places."

I turned my back to Clarissy for some privacy while I removed the corset. I was just slipping her undershirt over my head when I noticed Charlie looking up. As my eyes followed his gaze I notice Abraham and Doc Miller standing on the bank above me.

"Why you lecherous men! How long have you been standing there? Don't give me that adverting your eyes story either." I fumed. Clarissy ran to my aid covering me with my dress she had finished mending.

"Get, go on get, you've seen quite enough. You two should be ashamed of yourselves." Clarissy did her best to chase them off like stray dogs. Doc Miller was giggling like a schoolboy, but Abe seemed uncomfortable with the entire encounter.

"See how it feels when someone sneaks around and you don't know they're there?" Abe admonished as he and Doc Miller turned their backs and retreated a few paces.

"Abe, I'm sorry, I'm so sorry I didn't know. How could I have known and when you started explaining to Doc I just couldn't interrupt and then I realized I was being very rude and inconsiderate so I tried to leave and made a mess of everything. I am truly very sorry for your loss and for the pain my presence has caused you."

"Does that negro girl have you dressed yet?" Abe snapped.

"Her name is Clarissy, she has been kind and generous beyond reason. I would appreciate it if you thanked her and paid her for her undershirt that I am now wearing because you didn't see fit to get me a complete set of clothes. You also need to pay her for mending this borrowed dress and I would appreciate even more if you commissioned her to make me a dress of my very own. I would also like a pair of boots that fit. These have made blisters on my toes. And finally to answer your question, yes I'm dressed."

"Now look here Miss," Abe said turning to face me. "I did not take you to raise. I am a man of meager means who barely feeds and clothes himself. I can nary afford to have dresses made or buy you new boots. I owe you and that girl nothing!"

"Abraham, you need to hear what I am about to say and believe it. You are destined for greatness. You will change the world as you know it but only if you turn your back on the ugly practice of racism and slavery. You need to remember that this country was conceived in liberty and dedicated to the proposition that all men are created equal. You must judge people by the content of their character not the color of their skin. Do you understand? Somehow, someway I was sent here to ensure you understood this. I think if you start right now, with this woman, treat her like you would an equal, pretend you are blind, and see her for who she is not for what you think a colored woman should be. If you can do that I think I will be on my way home before she can finish with my new dress."

"Miss, I do appreciate what you are telling Mr. Lincoln but I am not a slave. I am a free black. I have no master. My father earned his freedom years before I was born. I get paid to do this laundry just like I would if I were white. I offered to mend your dress and give you my shirt neither you nor Mr. Lincoln owe me a thing. If you would like a dress of your own I would be happy to sew one for you if you would just bring me the materials. I fear to ask what has befallen you that would cause you not to have a stitch of your own clothing. Sewing a dress seems like the only Christian thing to do."

"Clarissy you are a fine Christian and thank you so much for keeping this poor confused woman safe and seeing to her needs. If you will come with me to the Mercantile we will get everything you need to make her a proper dress. I think Abraham should take Miss Catherine home for now and I will meet up with the both of them tomorrow."

Doc Miller took Clarissy by the hand and escorted her away from the creek toward town. I was still standing in my corset and petticoat with my dress on but still unbuttoned. I wasn't sure what I was supposed to do or say next. To my surprise Abe spoke first.

"Catherine, I have known you the better part of my life. As small children we played in this very creek together. I stood on that bank the first time I snuck a peek at you in your petticoat. I received a similar tongue lashing on that day. We were as close as two peas in a pod and most folks around here suspected we would eventually get married. I never requested your hand but I figured we would, someday. You kept me apprised of all your secrets and I was unable to keep a secret from you. We argued or as you called it debated about politics, slavery and the treatment of women. I garnered tremendous wisdom and insight looking at the world through your wild green eyes. Your soft and compassionate side was seldom seen but it ran deep into your soul. You also had a penchant for the taste of whiskey. I observed you stealing tastes from my glass and admonished you to which you replied those tastes were payment for the peeks at your petticoat I stole as a child. Without any realization I had fallen in love with you. It was easy, natural and not at all the burden men bluster on about. At just the point I felt I had acquired enough money, land, and standing in the community to start a family. You died! You left me alone in a cabin built for you, on land next to your kin, in a town you loved. If not for finding that stupid dog I would surely have followed. Now you have returned. Wearing a dress I borrowed from your sisters that once belonged to you. You have resumed lecturing me on racism and slavery. I want only one thing more than to walk away and never speak to you again, that is to beg you to marry me and fulfill my broken dream. I do so regret never asking for your hand when I had the chance."

With that Abe walked down into the creek and with trembling hands caressed my face. He looked so deeply into my eyes he could see my soul and I saw a tear form in the corner of his eye.

"You are not my Catherine," he whispered

"No, no I'm not. I wish I were. I wish I could somehow ease your pain but I can only offer you the hope for the future. I don't think you will ever recover from the loss of Catherine, but you will go on to do great things. Keep her in your heart, remember her side of the debate and by honoring that memory she will never truly be gone."

I reached up and brushed away the tear that was now falling. I kissed each of his cheeks like a mother comforting a child then slowly walked out of the river. Abe stood ankle deep in the water while I dressed and laced my boots. He didn't speak again until we reached the cabin.

Back at the cabin Abe went straight to tending the mules. I went inside and tried to make us some dinner. By the time Abe had finished with the mules I had made managed to make something that could pass for dinner. Charlie sat between us on the cabin floor while we silently ate. As soon as Abe finished his dinner he left the cabin and went back to the barn. I wanted to follow him but I knew the best thing I could do was give him some space. His heart was breaking and he needed some time. Since Abe was out of the cabin I decided to take the opportunity to freshen up a bit. I slipped out of my dress and corset and into Abe's nightshirt. I heated some water on the wood stove. I opted out of using any more soap; my skin was still raw from Clarissy's laundry soap. Plain hot water and a rough rag were going to have to do. I washed my hair and used just a tiny bit of lard in the palms of my hands as a detangling conditioner. Once I was clean I spot cleaned my dress again, washed my socks and then curled up in bed. Abe had several books in the cabin I picked one that looked interesting and lit the lamp on the nightstand. Charlie curled up next to me and suddenly everything seemed right with the world.

A Traitor Among Us

The phone woke me out of a dead sleep.

"Catherine, did I wake you?"

"Dad it's 6:30 in the morning and I was planning on taking the day off, so yes, you woke me."

"Charlie and I stopped at El Parasol to get some burritos and we were wondering if maybe Major Allen was around this morning and if so would he like a breakfast burrito."

"Major I think this is for you." I said shoving the phone under the Major Allen's pillow.

"Why yes, yes sir I would love a burrito. Thank you for thinking of me, no, no you didn't interrupt anything. As always, a pleasure sir. See you in just a few minutes. Great."

"You're so good with him. Why don't you ever tell him to mind his own damn business and leave us both alone?"

"Because you love your father and I love you. As annoying as it is that's his way of making sure he doesn't walk in on anything none of us want him to see. So rise and shine princess, the burrito man cometh."

"You can make a pretty good argument before coffee. Since you're so alert I think you should be the one to start the coffee and the shower while I stay in bed."

"Well played. Just remember your Dad and your newest love interest Charlie will be here in under twenty minutes so you better not get too comfy."

"Did I detect a little jealousy in your tone?"

"Maybe a little, I'm guessing he will have run of the house and be able to sleep in your bed whenever he wants."

"Oh you poor unfortunate soul, how I mistreat you so. Maybe you should just go to the garden and eat some worms."

"How about I just go to the shower before your Dad gets here and puts me to work?"

"Good idea he never makes you work if you have your uniform on."

"Is that your way of getting to see me in my dress blues?"

"You know I love a man in uniform."

Before I could manage to finish my first cup of coffee and get into my jeans Dad and Charlie were walking in the front door.

"Good morning Charlie. Did you and your Grandpa have a good day? I hope he hasn't spoiled you too much already." I said bending down and tussling him around.

"Ya know, he's a really smart dog," Dad chimed in. "He's house broke, he can fetch and play dead."

"Truckin' or Drivin' that Train?" Major Allen quipped as he entered the kitchen.

"Well, well, he looks smart and acts like a smart ass, must be a Major." Dad interjected.

"Good morning, Sir. Thanks for the burrito. I will have to take mine to go. Duty calls."

"Speaking of duty what did your guys find out yesterday about the gate and the iPod?" I asked as I walked the Major to his car.

"Strangely enough I got a phone call about that while I was in the shower. I don't know what's up but promise you will stay with your Dad and Charlie today or at least until I get some idea of what's going on."

"Sure, I have some reports to finish regarding the experiment. I was going to deliver them to LANL at some point today so I'll call you and let you know when I plan on leaving the ranch. Should I be concerned about any of this?"

"Now don't you worry about a thing Ma'am," the Major replied in his worst John Wayne impression while getting into his SUV.

"Cute, seriously what is our security level?"

"Don't be surprised to see some of my guys around the ranch and at the gate. That's all I can tell you right now. Just don't worry, I've got your back"

"Thanks, keep me up to date please. I know it's S.O.P. for us but it worries Dad."

I gave him a quick kiss through the window and then he was off. I couldn't help but wonder what he wasn't telling me, but that was a feeling I was all too familiar with.

"When are you going to make an honest man out of him?" Dad inquired.

"Leave it alone Dad, you know this never ends well, just leave it alone."

"He loves you and he could give you a good life if you would just stop pushing him away and insisting on living on this damned old ranch."

"And here we go, Dad I love you too but just like the Major, I don't want either of you around all the time. So thank you very much for seeing to my dog and for delivering breakfast. Now I think it's time you go back under that house that fell on you or wherever it is you came from this morning"

"Overreact much, do you?" Dad retorted without ever looking up from his breakfast.

"Meddle much?" I continued.

"Charlie, watch her when she gets like this. She's prone to being unpredictable."

"You think you can just talk to the dog and I'll forgive you?"

"Usually works, what's different about today?"

"I suppose nothing." I said as I sat down next to him and laid my head on his shoulder. "You know it's complicated between us. My career, his career, national security, oh yeah and let's not forget meddling parents. We have something that works and for now that's just going to have to be enough. I know you want what's best for your little girl Dad, but really I'm doing just fine. Now seriously, I have a huge report I have to work on so you are welcome to stay but I have to crawl into my hole of an office and not come out until it's done."

"How about Charlie and I go to the pet store and get him a kennel so he has his own bedroom to stay in while you're at work? Maybe by the time we're back you will have had enough coffee to improve your sunny disposition."

"Anything is possible Dad, anything is possible. Take my wallet and pick up the list of stuff from the feed store that's posted on the fridge while you're out."

"Anything else, your majesty?"

"No, that'll do Dad. Thanks, really, thanks for everything just give me some space until I finish this project."

"You know after this project there will be another and another until one day you realize you have put off your life until it's over."

"I know. But for today can I please just focus on finishing this report?"

"Finish your report then we will hitch up the team and see if your new dog will ride on a wagon. I bet he will"

"Deal. By the time you get back and get the team hitched I should be done with this and if I'm not I promise I'll quit anyway."

Dad did his best to keep me from becoming a work-a-holic. Some people might consider the work I did on the ranch as another job but Dad knew that for me it was a creative outlet. A place I could blow off some steam or build up a head of it. I always had something to work on and unlike at the Lab it was mostly physical work. My mind could rest for a while and when I did use it, I used an entirely different part. I think this is why I was able to find solutions other scientist missed. The project I was working on was a perfect example. I had picked up where another group of scientist had given up. They had not been able to see beyond what I found was a relatively simple problem. Now I was on the verge of providing the world with a sustainable, reusable energy source and clean drinking water. The report I was working on was giving the earlier scientist credit for their work while creating a clear boundary for where their work stopped and my work began. Of course there is never a clear boundary anywhere in science or nature but I felt I could provide enough empirical proof for this experiment to be fully credited to myself and my team. None of which mattered to me in the least but to the bean counters and the grant writers credit equals dollars and dollars are what in the end, fuels my research. I managed to put together a fairly decent report before Dad and Charlie returned.

"Did you know you know have a manned checkpoint at your gate?" Dad asked as soon as he came in.

"Yeah, the Major mentioned he might need to do that."

"Why, do you need men with guns guarding your gate?" Dad asked with the slightest panic in his voice

"Easy Dad, you know I can't talk about what I'm working on, but suffice it to say it's not a new recipe for Mac & Cheese but equally as unlikely is it anything dangerous or of the military variety. You know I don't do that so just relax and trust the Major who, like you, is just a touch overprotective. In his world, that means young men with guns watching over me. Consider it a sweet, complete waste of your tax dollars."

"Since I know there is no use arguing I'm going to go hitch up the team. Will you be down soon?"

"Yeah, I have a few graphs to add then I'll be right down."

Just after Dad left the house my phone rang and I could tell by the caller i.d. it was Major Allen. I had just been reaching for the phone to call him so as soon as I answered I started with:

"What the hell are you trying to do, give my father a heart attack? Could you have told your men to be a little subtle? This isn't a border crossing into whojawhatsitstan it's my goddam front gate!"

"Ms. Beaven if you are quite done, I would like to introduce you to the other members of this CONFERENCE call."

As Major Allen read off the list of participants which included members of the joint chiefs, the FBI, CIA and NSA, I thanked my lucky stars this wasn't a video call.

"Good afternoon, gentlemen." I began in my most professional tone. "May I first say what an honor it is to be working with all of you," I continued.

"Cut the crap Catherine, we know you hate having your little scientific world upturned by the brass, so let's get down to what our concerns are and what you're going to do to make sure your 1.2 billion dollar experiment doesn't fall into the wrong hands before we can recoup our investment."

"Yes sir, Mr. Secretary, and may I thank you for getting to the point. Now what intelligence, and I use that word carefully with this group, do you have to indicate there's any reason to be concerned?"

"Catherine you know we can't divulge our intelligence. All you need to know is we have a credible source that indicates you and your experiment have become the target of some sort of corporate espionage. We have not ascertained to what degree your research has been breached but we have reason to believe that there has been a significant enough breech to jeopardize your research and possibly your health."

"With all due respect you have no way of knowing what I "need" to know, but with that being said I think you should look very closely at the guards in the main lobby or my lab. More specifically, look into the guard who was on the left yesterday. I think he may be at least part of your leak."

"That is a very serious accusation do you have anything to substantiate it?" Major Allen interjected.

"As you are aware Major Allen I am unable to divulge my intelligence, all you need to know that I have credible intelligence that indicated your guard is dirty!"

"Thank you for your input Ms. Beaven. Please cooperate fully with Major Allen until this investigation is complete."

"Yes sir, Mr. Secretary. Now if that is all I have to go help my father."

"Yes of course thank you and good day."

I wasn't sure exactly how to feel when I hung up the phone. I appreciated the concern for my safety but I had a feeling any reason I had to be concerned somehow stemmed from having the military involved to start with. I went to the barn and helped Dad finish hitching the team. Dad had Charlie trained to jump up onto the wagon in no time so off we went. Dad drove and tried to keep the conversation going but my mind was elsewhere.

"You seem a little distracted, does it have anything to do with the boys at the gate?" Dad inquired.

"Yeah, Dad it does. Hey can you do me a favor?"

"Sure."

"Can you not come back to the ranch for a few days?"

"Sure, but why?"

"I don't really know, but I don't like having these guys crawling around and I don't trust that they won't shoot first and ask questions later. I think I may need to protect you from my protection. Can you keep close to your house for a little while? I'm sure this will blow over pretty quick but until then I'd just feel better if you were safe at home."

"Where are you going to be?'

"I think I'll take Charlie and stay at the lab for a couple of days. That place is safer than Fort Knox so there will be no need for either you or Major Allen to worry your pretty little heads."

"Lets get these horses back to the barn. I will head out after I feed tonight."

"If you're sure that's what you want."

"Yeah, I think it is for the best. I'll let the Major know when I am planning on leaving and I'm sure he'll send an escort. I'll call you in a couple of days and check in. Just remember, no news is good news."

Dad and I unhitched and unharnessed the horses then he headed home. He was a little reluctant but he trusted Major Allen to take care of me. I went up to the house while the horses cooled and packed a few things. It wasn't uncommon for me to stay in my lab. I had my own room up there and unlike the ranch it even had T.V. I could work on resetting my experiment while Major Allen and all his scary friends worked out whom, if anyone was trying to sabotage my project.

"Just a couple of days, Charlie." I said as I loaded him in my car. I stopped at the barn, turned the draft horses out and made a quick call to Major Allen.

"Are we on a conference call?"

"No, sorry about that but I tried to tell you and you wouldn't let me get a word in edge wise."

"I know, it's not the first or last time anyone on that call has heard me lose my temper. Anyway, I have Charlie and a few things in the car and I'm heading for the lab. I asked Dad to stay away from the ranch for a few days until all of this blows over. He put on a brave face but I could tell he was pretty worried. Promise me you won't let anything happen to that sweet old man."

"I promise nothing is going to happen to either of you. I figured you would want to come up here so there is an escort waiting for you at the gate. Once you get to the lab, I can come visit you if you would like?"

"Thanks but no. I have plenty of work to do and this is probably the excuse I needed to get it done. I'm sure I will see you in the morning. By the way have you changed that guard?"

"Yes, I reassigned him to someplace far away from you until I can finish my investigation. Are you going to share your intelligence with me or just make me figure it out?"

"I'll see what you come up with first then I'll help you out if you need it."

"You're all heart. I have to go. Be careful and call me if you think anything looks suspicious."

The drive up the canyon was uneventful and I was in my lab in less than an hour. Charlie seemed to like my room but he was having some trouble negotiating the polished concrete floors.

"Just slow down a little before the turn Charlie. Then you can accelerate out of the turn without crashing." I coached.

After Charlie mastered his cornering we turned in for the night. As I sat in bed with Charlie at my side, watching the late night news I mindlessly began fidgeting with his collar. Suddenly the gemstone in the center started to glow then it changed from green to amber.

"What the hell? Charlie let me see this collar of yours for a minute." I said taking Charlie's collar off his neck to get a closer look.

"What's this thing made of anyway? Hey look, there is a code on the gemstone. That wasn't there before. I wonder what that's all about."

My scientific brain had just been activated and I spent the next few hours going over every detail of Charlie's collar. In the end all I managed to figure out was I could change each digit of the code by touching the side stones in a certain combination. I had no idea what the code was for or how Charlie's collar was powered. It seemed to have an internal power source but I couldn't see any way of opening it. After a very thorough investigation I made a few notes in my journal and returned Charlie's collar to his neck. This was a problem for another day; Charlie and I needed some sleep.

"Come on Charlie, if we go to sleep right now we can get three maybe three and half hours of sleep before the Labbies show up."

Charlie and I snuggled into bed and were fast asleep in moments.

"Ma'am, Ma'am, I hate to wake you but we really need your help."

"Kevin, if there isn't someone bleeding and you don't have coffee I suggest you go away until one of those things happens. If you stay without coffee I can assure you there will be someone bleeding." I grumbled, hoping I could scare him off and get a few more minutes of rest.

"Ma'am, actually there is someone bleeding and I'm afraid things may get worse if you don't come quick."

"All right I'm up. Start talking while I get some clothes on."

As I jumped out of bed I realized the person bleeding was Kevin.

"Oh my God Kevin, what happened?" That's when I saw them. Two masked men in full military gear standing in the doorway just behind Kevin.

"Kevin, did these men do this to you?" I demanded.

"Yes Ma'am, but I'm fine or at least I'll be fine as long as you help me give them what they want."

"Where is the rest of my team, Kevin? I questioned as I slipped into the jeans and sweatshirt I had left on the floor by my bed.

"They have them locked in the containment environment for the experiment and they are threatening to evacuate the oxygen if we don't cooperate." Kevin was reaching a fevered pitch and I knew that panicked people seldom make good decisions. That's what the guys with the guns count on. That's the way they control situations.

"Kevin, look at me. Everything is going to be fine. There's nothing in this lab worth dying for so let's give the nice men what they want and get everyone safely out of that containment area. Okay? Kevin, look at me and say 'Okay'."

"Okay, Ma'am, it's just that our work, I'm so…"

"Kevin, stop! Stop that thought right there, right now your only thought is how to help these men. Helping them is how we get our colleagues out of that room. Do you understand? Nothing else, just give them what they came for and get the doors to that room open. Okay?"

"Yes, Ma'am"

I could see Kevin's panic ebb and his mind clear. He was beginning to think again and that was what I needed from him. He was of no use to me if he panicked.

"Now as for you two bullies. First off, keep your hands off my staff. If you want or need something act like big boys and use your words. I'm pretty sure you two goons aren't in charge so let's start by talking to whomever is running this show." I demanded as I headed for my door.

The goon on the left spoke first.

"Ma'am any lack of cooperation will be considered an act of hostility and treated as such. You are to take us to your lab, download your data onto our computer and then repeat your experiment so we can record the entire process."

"Wow, you are stupider than you look. That containment room you have my staff locked in is necessary to complete my experiment. So first off you will need to find a new jail."

The guard raised his hand as if her were going to hit me but I never flinched. I stood my ground never taking my eyes off him. I have learned a lot working with horses and one of those things is, never let them see you flinch. Make them question their behavior by just standing still. It's amazingly effective. As I stood staring into his eyes the other guard spoke up.

"Ma'am we will release all of your staff if you agree to cooperate."

"Look G.I. Joe. I am a scientist not a hero. I could care less what you do with my work but I swear I will use every means at my disposal to find each and everyone of you and bring you to justice, if you harm a single member of my staff. Do you understand me soldier?"

"Ma'am yes Ma'am" the soldier replied instinctively.

"Now get my people out of that room so I can give you what you want."

With that the two soldiers led Kevin, Charlie, and I to the lab. Kevin's nose was still bleeding and he was definitely going to have a black eye but otherwise he seemed fine. I stopped at the first aid station, grabbed some gauze and antiseptic and cleaned up Kevin's face.

"We don't have time for that." The solider protested.

"He can't go around contaminating everything with his blood. If you hadn't have felt the need to hit him we wouldn't have to stop and clean up your mess."

With that the soldiers left us alone for a few moments to radio their superiors.

"So this is Charlie?" Kevin asked rubbing Charlie on the head while I cleaned up his face.

"Not much of a guard dog, is he?"

"No, I guess not but he seems awfully smitten with you. You two looked pretty cute spooning in your bed until I had to wake you."

"I don't think it's called spooning when you're doing it with a dog. But anyway, how long have these guys been here?"

"A couple of hours maybe. It's really hard to tell. They waited until all the staff was in the lab then they killed the elevators and the communication. After that they took everyone to the containment room. They wanted to know whom you trusted the most and everyone pointed at me. I told them I wouldn't support terrorism. That's when the one guard slugged me and said I would do as I was told or he would kill everyone it that room. What was I supposed to do?"

"Easy Kevin, you haven't done anything wrong. I meant what I said; there is nothing in this lab worth dying over. Our job is to create; it's Major Allen and his boy's that are responsible for protecting. Let's just find a way to get these guys out of here without anyone getting hurt."

"I have to think they know you are the only one in the world who could recreate this. I'm afraid if we give them everything they will have no reason not to hurt you."

"Oh Kevin, they have no intentions of hurting me. They intend to kill me. I know that, but right now they will have to wait and for me that's a very good thing."

Kevin looked somewhat horrified and relieved at the same time. That's the trouble with geniuses: they never believe anyone else could possibly know as much as they do. Kevin didn't have to tell me these guys were here to kill me, I had figured that out all on my own but now that I had said it Kevin had to deal with the fact that these guys were here to kill me and very possibly him. I was hoping that realization would motivate Kevin to use that beautiful brain of his to find us a way out.

Charlie growled as the soldiers returned.

"You finally figure out they're the bad guys?" I asked Charlie as we started walking again.

"So Jarhead, have you set my people free?" I asked in my most sarcastic tone.

"Ma'am if you could refrain from speaking until spoken to this will go a lot smoother."

"Sorry, I've never been very good at that. So, how about you answer my questions the first time I ask and this will go a lot smoother." I repeat. "Has my staff be released?"

"Yes, they have been released and everyone is waiting in the lab."

"Thank you. See how easy that can be if we both just try a little."

Charlie was starting to get restless and I knew what that meant.

"Boys what is your plan for the dog?" I questioned as I stopped dead in my tracks.

"Ma'am you need to keep walking," one of the soldiers advised with a quick shove. I stood my ground.

"Charlie needs to pee. What is your plan for the dog?"

"With that one of the soldiers pointed his gun right at Charlie's head."

"If you do that this entire mission will fail." I said stepping in front of Charlie.

"The dog is not our concern, if he becomes a problem, we will eliminate him." The other guard said leveling his weapon at Charlie.

"I know your superiors don't give you grunts all the details but I would have thought they would have let you know what a high value asset Charlie is. If you kill him before we get to the lab and then you find out he is vital to your mission how are you going to fix that? Might I suggest you find a place for the dog to take a piss so we can get on with this."

"I think you're full of shit lady. That dog is nothing more than a pet."

"Are you willing to risk your entire mission to find out? Wouldn't it be easier to just take care of the dog? If I'm lying you can always kill him later."

Right then Charlie walked over and lifted his leg sending a stream of urine onto the soldier's boots.

"Well I see that problem has been resolved. Shall we continue gentlemen?" I quickly commented, hoping that would keep them from killing Charlie.

Thankfully it worked, and with pee dripping off his pant leg with every step the soldier led us into the lab.

My entire staff was crammed into my lab.

"Good morning everyone. Please tell me someone has made the coffee." To my compete surprise Major Allen stepped up and handed me a cup. He was wearing a lab coat and an id card that said Mark Bell.

"Thank you Mark, it's good to see you this morning." I said as smoothly as possible while looking for some hint to what was going on in the Major's eyes.

"I know you can't do anything before your coffee so I convinced these gentlemen to let me make some."

"Thanks, it's nice to see they're reasonable."

"All right then if all of you could step out of the lab except, Mark, Kevin, Lynn and Sanjay we will get these people what they have come for and get on with our morning."

"Listen lady, no one is going anywhere. I give the orders around here not you."

"Okay there Mr. Sunshine, apparently you and I have to get a few things straight." I started as I walked up toe to toe with him. "First, damn you're tall, what six-six, six-seven? Second, if you want this data and you want to steal my life's work then you are going to have to let me do what I do. You aren't robbing a bank here, this is a lab and we have protocol. Protocol that states, there shouldn't be any non-necessary personnel in the lab when actively conducting an experiment. As far as I'm concerned that means you, but I didn't figure I could get you to leave. But I sure as hell can send the rest of that lot out into the hall."

"There were additional personnel in this lab when you conducted your first experiment," the solider protested.

"How could you possibly know who was in this lab that day?" I demanded

"People, you heard the lady, out into the hall," the soldier directed hoping to distract me. As the soldiers herded my staff into the hall I made eye contact with Major Allen.

"You have a mole." I mouthed

"I see" The Major motioned back.

Once the lab was clear I had run out of stall tactics. I had Kevin begin to download of all my data onto their computer. This was an enormous project and the download would take quite some time. I had Lynn and Sanjay set up a small-scale version of our earlier experiment. It probably wouldn't yield enough energy to power the light or make anything more than some condensation but it would provide the appropriate data. I wasn't going to hand them everything. They would have to run the numbers and figure out how to expand this on their own. Major Allen and I sat at my desk adjusting the computer model. Kevin came over once he had the data downloading and made some lame but plausible excuse to use my computer.

"I need to ensure the program in the background is running properly." Kevin announced.

"Right, I always forget about that." I added for effect looking at Kevin for any indication as to what he was doing.

"That's why you're the boss and I'm the genius." Kevin retorted with a little sarcasm.

Kevin was a genius and with that comment I knew he had done something that would take another world-class genius to figure out. Suddenly I felt a little more optimistic about my future. As Kevin got up from my chair he mumbled a very important piece of advice.

"Stay away from metal." He said under his breath and looked at Major Allen as if I was supposed to relay that message. Just then Lynn and Sanjay returned from the setting up the experiment.

"Why don't you two join the others in the hall?" I asked.

"Now if you will bring your men inside." I directed the solider.

"I want to make sure you all see exactly what I am doing and realize that if this experiment fails it is not because of anything I have done."

The solider hesitated looking at the group of people in the hall.

"The walls are glass and you have guns. I don't think those people are going anywhere." I assured the soldiers.

"Now please watch the monitor carefully." I instructed as myself and Major Allen stepped away from the computers.

"Kevin, start the experiment."

Things started pretty much like normal. I watched the reading very carefully looking for some indication of what Kevin had done. I noticed that Kevin was very carefully removing all the metal from his pockets and his clothes. I quietly did the same and so did Major Allen. As I reached in my pocket to remove my keys I noticed they were warm, just slightly warmer than body temperature. That's when it occurred to me what Kevin had done.

"Oh he really is a genius. This is going to get interesting." I said under my breath.

I handed Major Allen my keys and looked him straight in the eye when I said

"If something happens to me I want you to have my smokin' red hot sports car." I saw the recognition in his eyes when he felt the warm keys.

This lab has an electromagnetic field that protects it from electronic spying. Kevin tapped into the field and re-calibrated it basically turning it into a giant MRI. Everything in this building that is made of metal was beginning to slowly heat up. I wasn't sure how hot the metal would get but hopefully hot enough to damage the processors and the hard drives on all the computers. As the soldiers began to fidget and sweat, I noticed an unintended consequence of Kevin's reprogramming. Not only were all the metals heating up there was a static charge building up, enough of a charge to make Charlie's fur stand on end.

This is getting a little dangerous. I thought to myself as I looked around at the bottles of compressed gasses stored across the room.

"One spark and things could get pretty sporty." Major Allen mumbled under his breath just loud enough for me to hear.

The good news was the soldiers were still focused on the download and the data stream, which were both starting to slow. Just then I heard Charlie whimper.

"Oh shit, oh no, hang on Charlie let me get that off you."

Charlie's collar was glowing and his fur was beginning to singe. I reached out and grabbed it without thinking and instantly got the shock of my life. My very next breath was filled with ice cold water.

"What the hell?" I tried to scream but I only sputtered.

I was being pulled under the water by the weight of my clothes. I instinctively started shedding clothes, shoes, jeans, sweatshirt, everything went until I was finally able to reach the surface. Just as I filled my lungs with air I felt my head slam into something hard. I fought to stay conscious but I was fading fast as the current eased and I drug myself onto shore.

There and Back Again

Charlie was standing on my chest waiting for my eyes to open.

"Subtle Charlie, real subtle," I groaned before ever opening an eye. Abraham was nowhere in sight but he had made a fire and hung my dress on the back of the chair in front of the stove to warm it before he left.

"Abe, you would have made Catherine a fine husband."

I commented to myself as I slipped into my nice warm dress. I opted out of the corset since it was just Abe, Charlie and I out here. Charlie was spinning himself in circles in front of the door wanting to go out. I stuck my feet in my boots but didn't bother to lace them so Charlie wouldn't have an accident in the cabin.

"All right, all right, Charlie I'm moving as fast as I can. Let's go see what today brings, shall we?"

I opened the door and Charlie was gone in a flash. I had learned it was no use to try to stop him when he ran off like that, or at least it was no use trying to stop my Charlie. I just assumed the same would be true here. I tried to keep my eyes on the general direction in which he disappeared and started walking. I had to stop and lace up my boots and strangely enough I was regretting not wearing the corset. The waist on my dress was painfully tight without it.

"Damned if I do, damned if I don't." I muttered referring to the corset.

"Excuse me, what did you say?" I nearly jumped out of my skin when I turned and found a strange man standing right behind me. Right behind him was Charlie.

"Where the hell did you come from?" I blurted out without thinking.

"Ma'am there is no call for vulgarity. It has been my intention to catch you for sometime. I feared if I called out I would frighten you and you would run."

"So sneaking up on me seemed like a better plan?"

"Well, yes Ma'am you didn't run."

"Fair enough. Who are you, what do you want and why have you been following me?"

"Clarissy said you was a little different. My name is Edgar; I am Clarissy's brother. She sent me here to give you this." Edgar held out his hand. He was holding a red dog collar, Charlie's dog collar. My Charlie's collar.

"Where did you get this?" I demanded as I snatched the collar from his hand.

"I caught it in the river." Edgar replied

"You CAUGHT it in the river, what are you talking about?"

"I was working on a flat boat on the river a few days ago. I always fish off the back of the boat while I work so hopefully by the end of the day I'll have somethin' for dinner. I saw my pole bend so I drug my catch into the boat. I was real disappointed when it wasn't anything I could eat. It looked like something a woman might like so I put it in my pocket to give to my sister. When I got back home I showed it to Clarissy and she told me I had to bring it to you first thing this mornin'. She was real sure it belonged to you and you needed it back. So here I am, a black man following a white woman through the woods with her property in his pocket. This is the way people get lynched in these parts. I'm sorry for sneaking up on you but it really did seem for the best."

"Thank you Edgar, and please tell Clarissy 'thank you' for sending this to me. Can I offer you some food or would you like to come sit and rest in the cabin for awhile?"

"No, Ma'am I need to get back and help our Pa. One of our mules has gone lame so he needs help with the plowing."

"Abraham has two fine mules, I'm sure he would allow you to use one for a day or two until your mule recovers. Let's go and find them. Then you'll have a ride back to town and a mule to help your father."

"That's real generous Ma'am but I sincerely doubt Mr. Abraham would let our family use one of his mules."

"Why? Are you violent with animals? Are you thieves or otherwise of low morals?"

"No Ma'am! We treat our animals real well and my family has never taken anything that wasn't theirs. We are however black, in case that had slipped your observation."

"I recognize the fact that you are black but I choose to see a human in need of something I can help them with. I can not guarantee Abraham will see things the same way but I can guarantee you will never get a mule you don't ask for."

With that Charlie and I started heading back to the cabin. Edgar followed, concerned, but hopeful.

"Abraham, Abraham!" I bellowed as we approached the cabin.

"Yes, Catherine over here with the mules." Abraham answered.

"Great, see Edgar this will be easy." I chirped.

"Abraham, do you know Edgar, Clarissy's brother?" I questioned as I entered the corral.

"No, I don't think I do. Nice to meet you." Abraham said with the tilt of his hat.

"What are you doing out here with the mules?" I questioned.

"It appears Jack is lame." He said with a frown.

"Can I give him a look?" I questioned as I bent down and felt Jack's fetlock.

"Why, I don't know if this is a safe place for a wo..." Abe started, but I shot him a look that made him quickly realize finishing that statement was not going to end well, so he turned to Edgar.

"Please thank your sister again for all her help yesterday. She is a very kind and generous woman."

"Abe," I interrupted. "It seems Jack has an abscess that is about to come through. I will be happy to soak his foot and tend to him while you take…what is your other mules name?"

"Daniel," Abe interjected.

"Of course it is." I chuckled "Anyway, if you would take Daniel to town for Edgar and Clarissy's father to borrow. Bring his lame mule back and I will doctor them both here."

"Catherine, what are you talking about? I can't let Edgar and his father work Daniel," Abe protested. Edgar started to say something but I jumped right in.

"Oh Abe, that is so kind of you to volunteer to do the plowing for Edgar's elderly father. I know you would take both your mules but since Jack is lame you will have to make a team out of your healthy mule and their healthy mule. Since you are such a good Christian man and setting such a fine example I would like to volunteer to nurse both your and Edgar's sick mules back to help. After all that would be, ONLY THE CHRISTIAN THING TO DO now wouldn't it ABRAHAM?"

I could tell Abe's blood pressure was on the rise but to his credit, he acknowledged that helping a neighbor in need was a kind and charitable act that could only serve the greater good and since his mule was also lame he may need the favor returned sooner rather than later. With the mule situation settled I sent Abe, Edgar and Jack to town. Abe protested a bit about leaving me alone at the cabin but I assured him that Charlie and I would manage just fine for a night or two. As soon as they were off for town I started working on a poultice for Jack's hoof. I found some pine tar in the barn, mixed in a little lantern oil and some wild herbs I was able to find close by and let the whole mess steep in one of my wool socks while I soaked Jack's hoof in some warm salt water. After a good soak I stretched my sock with the poultice over Jack's hoof and tied it on with a piece of twine.

"Pretty stylish Jack, it will be what all the mules are wearing before long." I teased. Charlie barked in approval.

Caring for horses and mules hasn't changed much since the Romans so I was pretty confident I would have Jack walking on all fours in no time. Charlie and I headed back to the cabin to see what we could find for lunch.

"Beans and Bacon it is Charlie. Not much variety around here but at least we won't go hungry. I found some cornmeal, flour, eggs and lard so we can have cornbread with our beans for dinner if I can figure out how to bake it." Charlie was too busy eating his bacon with a raw egg I had set out for him to be concerned about my plans for cornbread.

I sat down on the edge of the bed and began eating my lunch. I remembered I had stuck Charlie's collar in my pocket. I pulled the collar from my pocket and starting going over the last things I could remember before I ended up in the river. As I reviewed the events I mindlessly rubbed the collar between my fingers. Suddenly the gemstone in the center of Charlie's collar started to glow and change from green to amber.

What makes that happen? That's exactly what happened before it just suddenly started to glow. What causes this?

I sat there trying to think back to the only other time his collar had done this. It was the other night when I was sitting in my bed at the lab watching the news. Charlie was curled up next to me. I was stroking his head and fidgeting with his collar. Just like today, I was just rubbing it between my fingers when it lit up like a Christmas tree and changed from green to amber.

I had played with it for hours that night and figured out that there was a display in the gemstone that became visible once it turned Amber. It had a six digit alphanumeric code that I could change with the gems on the side but I never figured out what the code was for. I wrote down the code that it was set to when I first started fussing with it in case it was important. It seemed like a combination for something but I had no idea what. I still remember the code that was on it when I found it because it spelled out Charlie in alphanumeric. 3=C, Third letter in the alphabet, H, 1=A, R, 1, 5=E, 3H1R15 or CHAR1E. Okay, not exactly Charlie but close enough to make me think that the code was either important or a joke by a very smart person. Either way I hadn't forgotten it. The code was currently set to 3H2R11.

"What will happen if I set it back to 3H1R15?" I wondered out loud.

Charlie gave a quick bark and a wag of his tail.

"You approve, Okay mister smarty pants what next?"

I set the code in and the center and the gemstone changed back to green.

So rubbing it between my fingers seems to be what causes it to change colors. I changed the code the night before the accident while I was trying to figure how it worked. In the lab we had an enormous static build up just before the accident and Charlie's fur was standing on end and his collar was burning him. I remember reaching down to remove his collar... Think Catherine, Think, what color was the gemstone when you touched the collar? What color indeed?

I was completely lost in my thoughts when I heard something in the barn. Charlie and I left our lunch and went to investigate. We found Clarissy putting her fathers mule in next to Jack.

"Clarissy, it's good to see you."

"I see you couldn't manage your corset again."

"Wow, that obvious? I'm guilty as charged. Thanks for sending Edgar out with Charlie's collar. I think it is the key to solving my problems."

"That beautiful necklace is a dog collar?" Clarissy asked indignantly.

"A very special dog collar but yes, but a dog collar none the less. I'm glad you came by I wanted to ask you how you new it belonged to me?"

"Why Miss your name is on it. What did you think just cause I was black I couldn't read?"

"No, of course not. I assumed you could read but how did you know that I was Catherine Beaven?"

"At first I thought I must be wrong because, well you know Miss Catherine you're dead, or at least we all thought you died. Then Doc Miller explained they had faked your death because you had some rare medical condition. He said there was something wrong with your brain; they didn't want people to become a feared so they thought it would be best to pretend you were dead until they could find a cure or well, you really did die. The Doc said you were nearly better but you were still having some episode so he asked me not to tell anyone about seeing you. I promised I would keep it secret but when Edgar came in with your necklace I figured I should send him to bring it to you cause he never met you before and he can't read he wouldn't know he was keeping a secret."

"Thank you Clarissy for keeping my secret and for returning Charlie's collar."

"I still can't believe all that beauty is wasted on some old dog. I thought Charlie was the name of a Beau or someone special, not a dog."

"Charlie is no Beau but he is a very special dog and worthy of a very special collar. You see the gemstone in the center of this collar? Watch, it changes colors when I rub it between my fingers."

Right as the gemstone started changing colors I realized I had changed the code, now I was activating the collar again.

"Oh dear, Clarissy I think I may have gotten carried away with myself. If I disappear please don't be frightened. I will be just fine. Please tell Abe and Doc Miller what happened and that I am fine. I will find a way back soon. Clarissy don't be frightened everything is…"

"Going to be okay. Dad for the last time don't feed that dog ice cream it gives him gas" I finished my sentence and realized I was standing in the kitchen at my Dad's house.

Dad dropped his container of ice cream and grabbed me giving me the biggest hug of my life, while Charlie jumped in circles then began eating the ice cream dad had dropped.

"You're not dead, you're not dead!" He exclaimed.

"No, no I'm not dead."

"What happened? Where have you been? How did you get here and why are you dressed like that?"

"You first, what happened? What day is it and would you please put on some pants? I can't believe I caught you in the middle of a midnight ice cream binge."

Dead and Gone

Dad and I spent the rest of the night going over what had happened. He had been told by LANL that there had been an accident in my lab resulting in death. They were unable to release my body due to "Matters of National Security" but they extended their condolences for his loss. Dad wasn't buying the whole thing but he did believe that something terrible had happened to me and that I was dead. Major Allen had come by to see him and indicated that LANL may be covering something up, but I was indeed gone. What Dad didn't understand was there is a big difference between dead, and gone.

I did my best to explain that no matter what he saw, I had not been resurrected on the third day in his kitchen. Really, I had never died.

"Sorry Dad, there will be no beatification for me. I did not die so it is not a miracle that I came back. I know you have always wanted an audience with the Pope but honestly this is not a miracle. It is however, a very astounding discovery that there is another planet or time or dimension or whatever it is, that we can access without the need for space travel. Or maybe I did travel through space… whatever happened I went there and back with barely a scratch. Had I managed to arrive on dry land I think the trip would have been considered a non event."

"Non-event? You were rescued by Abraham Lincoln. Pre Civil War, Abraham Lincoln." Dad exclaimed.

He was pretty worked up over the entire event, which was understandable but very out of character. This was a man whom I'd never seen panic and whom I had seldom seen show any emotion above mild interest. I could tell the past three days had taken a significant toll on him so I tried to focus on the positive aspects of what had happened.

"Dad, I'm really sorry you thought I was dead. I wish that had never happened. Please realize I am fine, I am here, in your house with you. I know what happened and I know why it happened which means I can predict and or prevent if from ever happening again. No more surprise vanishing acts, I promise. This is a very powerful technology and I would like to study it. That means I will probably leave again, but not before I work some things out and definitely not without telling you what I plan to do."

"Thanks, I'm sorry I got excited but you know you are the only thing I have left, and when they came and told me you were gone, well I really didn't handle it well. I didn't feel like you were gone, not like I did when your Mom passed but I just figured I must be in denial. Then Major Allen came by and he was all broke-up, he said he was there when the accident occurred and you were definitely gone. Everyone kept saying you were gone I just assumed that meant dead."

"Ah Dad, you should know there is a big difference between dead, and gone" I said with a wink. This got the first chuckle out of him since we started talking.

I explained to Dad I had figured out that Charlie played a very important role in all this and until I could figure out exactly what his role was no one, absolutely no one was to know anything about Charlie or his collar. As far as everyone was concerned, this must have had something to do with my Biomass experiment. Dad wanted me to quit the Lab and stay on the ranch. He was understandably shaken by the entire event and desperately wanted to keep me safe and at home.

"Dad I have to go back to work. I have to figure out how Charlie's collar works and where I went. I need to know if this is time travel, space travel or dimensional travel. I have to figure out how it ended up here and why my name is on it. There could be another father out there looking for his daughter and suffering through the same things you have just been through. I have to have some answers. I promise I will be very careful and please, promise me you won't breathe a word of this to anyone."

"I promise. Not a word, I will do anything to keep you and Charlie safe. How are you going to explain this at work? The resurrection story isn't sounding that bad now, is it?" Dad prodded.

"The resurrection story is still a bad idea but I don't really have a good one. I could tell them aliens abducted me. This is New Mexico right? How about teleporting? The energy build up teleported me about a three days walk from here."

"I know! Invisibility, you were there all a long. They just couldn't see you."

"Oh, ya know Dad, you may be on to something. I think I may be able to convince them that on a quantum level I was just slightly out of sync due to the unstable environment around my test. So in essence I was invisible. The effects lasted three days and now I'm back."

"Do you think they'll buy it?"

"At the very least they will send me for some tests that I will be real curious to see the results of. And what are they going to do? Argue with the fact that I am standing in front of them when they all watched me disappear?"

"That's my girl, plausible deniability. Just ask them who they're gonna believe, you or their lying eyes?" With that we both busted up laughing.

"Thanks Dad, I needed a good laugh. I'm exhausted, I really need a shower and I would love some clean clothes. Do I have a pair of jeans over here?"

"Yeah, I have a pair of your jeans and a sweatshirt from when we went camping. I'll get them while you shower. Would you like a cold beer?"

"Actually I would love some Bourbon, do have any Knob Creek? I feel like toasting Abe."

"You want it the usual way?"

"Yup, three fingers on the rocks with a twist. Hold the ice and the fruit."

"I'll make your drink. You get in the shower. We can toast Abe after you smell a little sweeter."

A hot shower is one of the most overlooked, under appreciated modern advancements. Sure vaccines are good, the automobile is handy but a hot shower is ten minutes of pure self-indulgence. There is no substitute for fresh hot water pouring over your tired body with just enough pressure to achieve the softest of massages. I had nearly run the hot water heater dry when I heard Charlie bark.

That's odd who would be here in the middle of the night?

That's when I took note of the sun peeking through the bathroom window.

Okay, so it very early in the morning, I corrected myself, but nonetheless, who's here?

I grabbed a towel and headed for the kitchen. I could hear Dad and another man talking. The voice seemed concerned that Dad was mixing a drink at this hour in the morning.

Sorry Dad, I thought to myself.

It wasn't until I was almost to the kitchen I realized who was there and why. It was Major Allen; he had come to take Dad to my memorial service.

Wow, is this going to be awkward.

I stood in the hall. Dad had convinced the Major to share a drink with him in my honor.

I guess this is my cue.

I screwed my courage up and walked into the kitchen, dripping wet, wearing only a towel. It was like a scene from a movie. The Major looked up at me, his mouth and his hand opened simultaneously, before he could utter a word the glass he had be holding shattered on the kitchen floor.

"Ta-Da," I exclaimed as Dad gave me the stink eye.

"You couldn't wait until he had finished his drink could you?" Dad rebuked.

"I know it's a sin to waste Bourbon but it would have been worse if he had gotten it up his nose."

"Fair enough. Now go get dressed while we clean up this mess. I think the Major may need a minute and another drink."

"Major, I'll be right back." I assured him as I went back down the hall.

By the time I was dressed, Dad and the Major had cleaned up the broken glass and were both enjoying a fresh round.

"I see I'm already behind. I think drinking before breakfast is one of the signs of alcoholism isn't it?"

"Seeing my dead girlfriend before breakfast may also be a contributing factor to alcoholism but I have to admit I'm damn happy to see you." The Major said as he pulled me onto his lap.

"Girlfriend? What is this high school? I haven't been anybody's girlfriend for twenty years. See what happens when you die, people start revising history and turning you into a saint."

"Well I see death didn't mellow you any. Okay, woman I occasionally take to dinner and enjoy her company in a carnal way. What the hell happened and where have you been."

"That's better. See how easy it is to just tell it like it is? I said with a sarcastic smile and a wink.

"Well if it's all right with you two love birds, I'm going to call and cancel the memorial service before anyone says anything

102

nice about Catherine, then Charlie and I are going to bed. I haven't stayed up all night since you were in college and I really prefer not to do it again. Now Catherine, do you think you could please manage to keep yourself visible or whatever the hell you call what happened to you until I get up?"

"Yes Dad, I'll be here when you get up and thanks. I'm real sorry for the scare and I promise it will never happen again. Get some rest. I will debrief the good Major and then I think I'll hit the hay too. It's been a rough couple of days and I could use some rest."

Dad wandered off down the hall with Charlie in tow. His age showed in his gait when he was tired. I really felt bad about the stress this had caused him but I hoped he would be okay after some rest and a good cuddle with Charlie.

Now I needed to turn my attention to Major Allen. I wanted to tell him everything that I had told Dad but I knew that wasn't a good idea. I also needed to know what happened in my lab after I disappeared and I knew he probably wouldn't or couldn't tell me. Military men often put their country and the military above themselves and their families. That's how they manage to do the things they do. That is also why I refused to be Major Allen's "girlfriend". I contended that he already had a significant other in his life and I never competed with anyone or anything for a man. As long as he was active military I would never commit to him and him alone because he couldn't do the same for me. It had worked for us for a long time but I could tell this was going to be the biggest challenge our relationship had ever faced.

"Tom" I started.

"Tom! You never call me Tom. This can't be good. I've known you for fifteen years and I can only think of two occasions when you've used my first name. What the hell happened to you?" The Major demanded in a very agitated tone.

"TOM," I started again. "I am going to tell you everything I can about what happened. You need to understand that I can't tell you everything. I probably shouldn't be talking to you or Dad at all until I am properly debriefed. I also know you can't tell me what happened the day I disappeared until I am debriefed. I do believe both of you deserve some explanation. I know most of the last three days will be considered top secret material that quite frankly is above both of our pay grades and security clearances so once I am debriefed I'll never be able to explain any of this. I need you to know I am not keeping anything from you that is relevant to our relationship. For once, right now, I need you to be Tom, not Major Allen just Tom. Can you do that?"

"Wow! This is rich. I have been begging you for ten years to let me leave work at work and come home to you. I have tried to explain to you that I could be both Major Allen and Tom but no, you're an all or nothing kind of gal, so I've settled for whatever you call our screwed up arrangement just to keep a relationship with you. Now after I've watched you vaporize in front of my eyes, after I've come here to notify your father of your death, after I've suffered through being denied any information about the accident because we've done such a good job of hiding our relationship, after I've spent most of this morning weeping like a child so I won't have any tears to shed for you in public and after I've come here to provide a military escort for your father to YOUR memorial service only to find you are alive and well, after all this you have the nerve to ask me if NOW I can be just Tom. No, no I can't be just Tom. Catherine, you can't have it both ways anymore. I'm Major Tom Allen, I have been in love with you since the day we met and I'll love you until the day I die. I have honored your memory and mourned your death, NOW I'm ready to move forward, everything from this moment on is new. The old rules don't apply. We are either in this together or not at all. I understand there are things you may not be able to share just as there are things I will not be able to share but our lives, our feelings, our commitment to one another is not something I can or will hide ever again. Catherine Elizabeth Beaven do you love me?"

"Yes, I love you. That has never been the question, and I know you love me but how do we share our lives with a horde of monster secrets between us?"

"By focusing on the things we know to be true."

"If you say life, liberty and the pursuit of happiness I swear I'll puke."

"No, how about the fact that after all this time we always end up right here."

"On Dad's sofa?"

"No, right here with each other, supporting, loving and protecting each other. Catherine you always make things harder than they have to be. We have been in a committed, monogamous, long term relationship for years you are just too stubborn to admit it."

"So if it's working so well, why change? If it ain't broke don't fix it, right?"

"You were the one who led with 'Tom'. What changed? What happened to you that makes you so afraid of the military? Why are you afraid I'll have a conflict of interests and why do you believe that whatever happened will cause a conflict between us?"

"God I hate the fact that you know me better than any other human on the planet. Do you want the truth? Well you can't handle the truth." I said in my best Jack Nicholas impression.

"You're really making a joke right now?"

"Did you really think I would pass up a reference to 'A Few Good Men'?"

"No, I guess not. I guess that also reassures me that you weren't replaced by an android because surely they could have programed a better Jack impression than that."

"Cheeky today aren't we? Which stage of grief is sarcasm? I always forget. Anyway back to the truth. Honestly I've never been afraid of whether or not you'd choose me over your career, the military or national security. I've always been afraid that you wouldn't. This country needs men who are willing to make tough decisions and endure the consequences of those decisions. You are one of those men. I know your tours in places that shall remain unnamed were difficult choices but would you've been able to make them with a wife and family? How many ops have you been assigned to that married men weren't eligible? What would you have given up if I had of accepted that ring ten years ago?"

"What ring? I have never proposed to you?"

"No, you haven't but you have been carrying a ring in you inside jacket pocket for over a decade." I said as I reached in his pocket and pulled out a small black velvet bag, tied with a red satin ribbon.

"Why didn't you ever say anything if you knew?" He said putting the bag back in his pocket.

"What was I going to say? You never asked the question."

"I was never sure you would accept. I was afraid if you said no we would split up."

"I think deep down you were afraid of the same thing I was. You aren't a corporate climbing accountant and I'm no soccer mom. Our situation is unique, I think all and all we have managed it pretty well. That is until I up and died in front of you. That tends to shine the harsh light of reality on what's important and what's not. I'm just afraid we may not have seen the same things in that light."

"Maybe we did, maybe we didn't, but we will never know if you don't trust me enough to explain to me what happened and why you are so afraid."

I knew Tom was right but this whole conversation had given me a headache and the bourbon had relaxed me just enough all I really wanted to do was take two aspirin and go to bed.

"Tom. Can we go back to where this conversation started? Can you, for just one morning, please just be Tom for me? I need someone to hold me while I sleep, bring me tea and biscuits when I wake up and for one day pretend we are a normal happy couple enjoying a lazy day in bed. Can you do that?

"Yes Catherine, I can today. How about I put you to bed, get you some water and aspirin and promise to be right beside you when you wake up."

"That would be just splendid. How did you know I needed some aspirin?"

"You have a tell when you are in pain."

"Really, you never mentioned it before."

"I've spent a lot of time thinking about all the little things you do over the past three days."

"I'm sorry for that. I really didn't mean for that to happen and I promise it will never happen again."

"I know, now lets get you to bed before you fall over."

"Before I go to sleep. You did get the bad guys didn't you?"

"Of course I did and all of your staff are just fine thanks to you and Kevin."

"Thanks for that, Good night, Tom."

Namaste

"I am a scientist from the United States of America." I began my explanation to Heinrich and Peter very slowly.

"Ya, ya we know you are an American. How did you get here?" Heinrich questioned again.

"I have been working on a project that allows me to pass between dimensions."

"Dimensions? I do not understand, what is a dimensions?" Peter quizzed.

"This planet we live on exists simultaneously in hundreds, possibly thousands of different dimensions. Think of it like a house of mirrors. If you were to place an object, let's say the Earth in the center of a room full of mirrors it would be reflected into infinity. Now if you were to walk around that object, the Earth, every step you take around it in the room would change what you see in the mirrors. But the object hasn't changed. The only real change is your perspective. Each dimension exists in the mirror not on the object. This is why they can occupy the same time in space. I have devised a way to travel between the images in the mirror or dimension as I call them. Because each dimension is essentially a reflection they are pretty much the same but the lives of the people and the progress of society and technology happens in each dimension at it's own rate. Time remains constant but not equal, if that makes any sense at all."

Heinrich and Peter looked very confused. They started speaking in German then arguing in German until finally they both looked at me and Heinrich asked again.

"So how did you end up HERE? Or maybe why did you end up here?"

That was a much more complicated question than either of them could have ever imagined and one I was very reluctant to answer honestly or completely.

"I'm not exactly sure. I am still experimenting with this process and I haven't worked out all the answers yet. What I do know is that I generally end up somewhere I can be useful and I never stay too long. So tell me about yourselves, what you are doing in this far corner of the world and how I can best be of assistance to you."

Neither of the men seemed satisfied with my explanation but they both seemed to realize they probably wouldn't ever understand and really it wasn't that important anyway. Heinrich jumped up and announced,

"You are poorly dressed for this climate. Peter has a friend, a seamstress. Let's get you some clothes and find a way for you to be useful."

I had to admire his style. No sense focusing on problems let's focus on doing something instead. So with that, the three of us headed into town.

The village was small but quite busy. There was a butcher shop, a mercantile, a bicycle repair shop, and up on the hill there was a temple. A majestic looking place with what appeared to be a golden roof.

"That's impressive." I said pointing to the temple

"Yes, this is the sacred city of Lhasa and that is the temple of the Dali Lama." Heinrich informed me

"How can you not know where you are?" Peter asked in a somewhat annoyed tone.

"Peter, Can we just forget about how I got here and focus on how I can leave?" I asked as politely as I could

"If you're leaving why are we having clothes made for you?"

"I don't know, Peter, ask Heinrich."

"She looks like a gypsy and she is wearing my socks and your sweater. I do not know about you but I would like my socks back. Besides it gives us good reason to see that pretty seamstress girl you want to ask on a date. Maybe this time you will speak." Heinrich said slapping Peter on the back.

As we walked I realized I was having a difficult time keeping up. My head was starting to hurt and I was feeling a little ill.

"Gentlemen" I shouted as I stopped and bent over.

"The altitude" The both said simultaneously

"Yes, the altitude. Any chance of some water, aspirin and a short rest?" I asked still bent at the waist trying to catch my breath.

"We are nearly to the seamstress shop, she will make us some tea and you can rest while Peter explains your situation. Peter is fluent in the local language yet somehow he can hardly speak a word to our lovely seamstress friend. This will be good. Now come on, just a little further." Heinrich said as he ducked his head under my shoulder nearly picking me off the ground as he stood.

Heinrich was like a force of nature. There was no stopping him or even slowing him down. His energy was contagious and impossible to ignore. My head was hurting, I was on the verge of vomiting and yet walking arm in arm with Heinrich I was smiling.

"Let's get you inside before you collapse," Peter commented while helping me into the seamstress's shop.

Inside the shop a beautiful young woman sat me on an exquisitely ornate pillow and handed me a piping hot cup of tea. I was having great difficulty focusing, but everything in the shop seemed so beautiful. The colors were so rich and vibrant and the smell of sweet incense hung in the air like honeysuckle on a humid summer evening. As I sat and drank my tea, Peter conversed with the young lady in the local language while Heinrich sat with me. Heinrich seemed very pleased to see his friend talking with the young lady. I think he was playing matchmaker. As my mind started to sharpen I noticed the temple out the window again.

"Did you say we are in the sacred city of Lhasa?" I asked Heinrich.

"Yes, this is Lhasa and the only way I know to get here involves a very long trek so I'm still confused as to how you could possibly not know where you are."

"The Dali Lama lives in the temple?" I continued ignoring Heinrich's question.

"Yes, or at least the current incarnation of the Dali Lama."

"Is the current incarnation a small child?"

"Yes, he is, eight maybe nine. Why do you ask?"

"I think I may know how I can help you."

"I am having new clothes made for you and you are the one doing the helping?"

"Yes, I am going to help you. Have you met the Dali Lama?"

"No, I am a foreigner so I am not allowed to meet the Dali Lama."

"You are if he requests it. So we just need to get him to request an audience with you."

"Why do I want to meet the Dali Lama?"

"Because he will provide you a valuable service someday and you will provide him an education which he can't get from anyone else in Lhasa."

"How do you know this?"

Just then Charlie stood in the window and let out a bark.

"What's out there Charlie?"

Out the window I saw a procession passing by. There were dozens of young monks all dressed in red walking and chanting in front of a gilded carriage being carried by six very large very strong monks dressed in red robes with golden sashes. Inside the golden carriage sat a small boy. He sat staring straight ahead without any sign of emotion. As the carriage passed, all the local villagers bowed their heads. As Heinrich, Charlie and I stood staring out the window the carriage stopped. The small boy turned and looked directly at the three of us. I realized we had broken protocol; we should've never made eye contact with him. Without thinking I ran for the door grabbing a white scarf off the wall on my way out. As I broke out onto the street I caused and enormous stir. Monks were yelling, women were screaming and I was focused completely on the small boy in the carriage. Right as I reached the side of the carriage I was accosted by two monks. They grabbed both my arms and wrenched them behind me I fell to my knees. I was still grasping the white scarf in my hand. I lifted my head and looked into the eyes of the small boy.

"Namaste," I said.

The boy looked very surprised. He motioned for the monks to allow me stand. There was some argument between the monks, the boy, and his advisers, but eventually I was allowed to stand. I took the scarf, folded it gently and offered to the small boy. He in turn unfolded it and placed it around my neck. No one in the village was speaking or even breathing while this exchange took place. I bowed my head respectfully and backed slowly away from the carriage. As soon as I was clear, the boy had a quick word with one of his advisors then the carriage began to move quickly up the street towards the palace. I walked back in the shop where the young woman, Peter and Heinrich all stood with their mouths open.

"What? I suppose you think I have made an egregious error." I asked sitting back down on the pile of pillows.

"Yes, you have made a very egregious error." Peter nearly shouted. He was pacing, staring at me, rubbing his head and pacing some more.

"What did you say to him?" Heinrich asked in a much kinder tone.

"What difference does it make Heinrich? This woman has just gotten us thrown out of Lhasa. I'm sure of it. What were you thinking?" Peter continued his tirade.

"I said Namaste." I told Heinrich

The young woman looked up and nodded.

"That was very good," she said in somewhat broken English.

"Why Namaste?" Heinrich wanted to know.

"It is Indian, but it is used in Tibet and Nepal also. It means 'I bow before you'. It is usually said by youth to an elder. By saying it to the young boy I was showing him I respected him. We had made eye contact through the window and I knew that was considered disrespectful. I couldn't let our first interaction end with disrespect so I did what I thought was best, I offered him a Khata so he could in turn give it back. This along with the Namaste let him know I was properly contrite for inadvertently breaking protocol."

"You do realize what you did can be considered treasonous behavior and they could have beheaded you in the street?" Peter asked.

"Yes, Peter, I do and I'm sure there were some in that group who would have done so without a thought but I knew that young boy would forgive me of my transgression if I allowed him a graceful way to do so."

"I like her. She is bold, strong and fearless," Heinrich said placing his hand on my shoulder.

"She may be too bold." Peter said pointing to the monk walking in the door.

The monk was holding a letter addressed to the 'foreign woman'.

"I guess this is for you," Peter said looking at the letter.

In perfectly written English the letter said:

You and your two foreign companions are requested to attend an audience with the Dali Lama this evening at sunset.

That was all. No reply to, or by, or option to not attend. It was as though it had been copied from a prior invitation.

"So how quickly can you make me a proper outfit I asked the young woman?"

Peter translated and the young woman immediately started taking my measurements.

"One hour, maybe two." The young woman said to me

"You need to bathe," She added quickly.

"Where does a girl get a hot bath?" I asked both Heinrich and Peter.

"There is a bath house in town. I will take you over there while Peter stays and helps out our young seamstress. When your outfit is complete, Peter can deliver it to you so you will be ready in time to meet with the Dali Lama."

I wasn't the least bit surprised to find this was a public bathhouse. Heinrich's willingness to go with me seemed a little less altruistic now. The water was extremely hot and the steam was as thick as the fog over San Francisco Bay so voyeurism was kept to a minimum. After a good scrubbing by one of the attendants I joined Heinrich in the soaking tub.

"This doesn't offend your European sensibilities?" I questioned.

"It did at first but now it seems nice. All people are equal here. Everyone needs a place to bathe and creating a communal place to do it makes the most sense. Besides I would never have the patience to get my water this hot."

"It is hot and it does feel good. Is there ever any... well inappropriate behavior in here?"

"No, these are very kind and respectful people. You have children, mothers, grandmother, everyone here at the same time so all social rules apply."

"That's nice, no objectifying women."

"You are a very interesting woman. You are worried about being looked at by men, yet you waltz into the street and introduce yourself to the Dali Lama."

"Being objectified is very different than being looked at."

"Can I do both?" Heinrich asked with a little boy smile.

"No, you need to mind your manners and listen to what I am going to tell you. You need to engage the Dali Lama at our meeting tonight. It is very important that the two of you become friends."

"Why would the Dali Lama befriend me and why do you think it is important?"

"Remember what I told you about the mirrors? Well the earth reflected in each of the mirrors is happening at the same time but time is not happening the same way in each of those reflections. Think of it this way. 'Time and space are just modes of how we think not conditions of how we live' a great man said that or will say that. Anyway, I have theorized that there are events that need to occur in each of the mirrors before that reflection can move forward. Take the discovery of fire, humanity can't move out of the cave until they master fire. In one reflection humans discover fire a thousand years after the Earth is formed in another one it takes two thousand years. Just like there are key events there seem to be key people. Jesus, Buddha, Mohammed, Churchill, Abraham Lincoln and the Dali Lama just to name a few. For some reason these people show up in every reflection. You, Heinrich, are connected to the Dali Lama on a quantum level. I know you have no idea what that means but what it means to me is that the two of you need to be brought together in order for this world to move forward. I wish I could explain it better but I have only recently developed this theory and I'm still working out a lot of the details. Please just trust me and know I have no reason to lie to you or do you any harm. Besides you are ruggedly handsome. Who wouldn't want to befriend you?" I added with a little smile.

Heinrich smiled back but seemed a little uncomfortable when the tables were turned.

"Why are you trying so hard to be a matchmaker for Peter?" I asked trying to relieve the awkwardness.

"Peter is a man who needs a wife. Some men need wives while others just need the company of women."

"Really? Please explain."

"I think it's true for women too, it's just harder for them because they are supposed to need a husband. I bet you don't have a husband in whatever reflection you come from, do you?"

118

"Not exactly, but I do have the company of a good man."

"That's not the same. I have often shared the company of a good woman but I have never married. Peter has seldom had the company of any woman but I'm sure he will marry. His soul needs it, mine does not and I bet your soul is like mine saved only for yourself.

"Maybe it can change, maybe it will change. I don't know, but right now my soul is content, how about yours?"

"My soul is dirty and ready for a bath if you will take your new dress so I can get cleaned up before it's time to go." Peter interrupted.

"Right, thanks for the delivery service Peter. I guess that's my cue to leave." Peter was standing holding a towel outstretched. He politely looked away as I got out of the tub and once I had wrapped myself in the towel he handed me a stack of beautiful silk.

"How do I put it on?" I asked.

"There is an attendant for the ladies where you came in she will help you." Peter instructed as he slipped into the tub.

"Will I ever end up anywhere I can dress myself?"

Matter of National Security

"I realize my ID has been invalidated and yes I know your records indicate that I am deceased, but as you can clearly see I am not. I have a meeting with the Deputy Director in five minutes and I'd really hate to be late so would you please just call her office? She is expecting me."

"Ma'am I have contacted security and they will be here any moment to deal with you."

"Deal with me, I don't need to be dealt with I need to go to a meeting. Does your supervisor know about your sterling customer service and amenable attitude?" I fired off as the security detail arrived.

"What seems to be the problem here?" the officer asked the gentlemen at the front desk. Without so much as looking up the gentlemen pointed at me and said,

"She's not dead but the lady whose ID she is using is."

With that he went back to reading his email or whatever he was doing on his computer.

"Ma'am could you please come with us, we will need to sort this out. Trying to gain access to a secure facility with a fraudulent Id is a serious crime."

"Officer, Bob, Tom, whatever you name is, my ID is not fraudulent, I have security clearance way, way above your pay grade and unless you pick up a phone and call the Deputy Director to let her know I'm here and that you're the one keeping me from our meeting the only security job you will ever hold in this town again will be guarding the Sonic. Now call the Deputy Director or make Mr. Mary Sunshine over there give me back my cell phone and I will call her myself."

"Wait right here for just one second." The officer walked away a few feet and radioed his office to call the Directors Office. Within a few moments I heard a familiar voice come over the radio.

"Officer, thank you for your diligence. I'm afraid it hadn't occurred to me that Ms. Beaven's ID had been deactivated. Please escort her to my office."

"Thank you Ma'am, I'll bring her up personally."

"I'd prefer to ride the elevator alone, but I completely understand you needing to do a little damage control," I barbed.

"I don't care who you are or what you want, I told the Deputy Director I would escort you so that's what I'm doing."

As I stood in the elevator I could feel the tension in my body rising. I had thought a lot about the day of the accident and ending up in Kentucky, but as I stood shoulder to shoulder with an unknown man in uniform, I realized how scared I'd been that day and how close I really came to ending up dead. Major Allen and I hadn't talked about what happened after I disappeared, other than he got the "bad guys". The Deputy Director had set up my debriefing so hopefully I would be leaving her office with most of my questions answered. I however, had no intentions of answering too many of theirs.

The elevator doors opened into the marble foyer of the Director's suite I breathed a sigh of relief. The director was seldom on sight, he was usually in Washington securing funding so the Deputy Director, for all intensive purposes, ran LANL. She was an old college friend who had been a loyal ally to my projects and myself. She knew I was lousy at politics but my work was world class. I was able to cut through all the bureaucratic red tape with her, which was why I had come to New Mexico and why I had stayed.

"Allison, sorry I'm a little late." I said looking directly at my escort.

"No problem, Thank you officer for seeing Ms. Beaven up. Please ensure her ID card is reactivated and have the front desk send up her phone."

"Yes, of course Ma'am, right away."

As Allison and I walked down the hall to the conference room she stopped and gave me a huge hug.

"That's out of character."

"Oh, Shut up and enjoy it, it's the only one you will probably ever get." she said wiping away a tear.

"Hey, Allison, I'm fine. I have always been fine. I disappeared, I didn't die."

"That would have been useful information to share with the rest of us."

"I did my very best to reappear, reanimate, reconstitute, or whatever you want to call it. And might I add, I was successful. I'm sorry it took three days but really I think that's pretty impressive."

"I know you're right, but for me it was three days planning how to bury one of my oldest and dearest friends."

"I really am sorry for everyone that was hurt by this. I will do everything in my power figure out what happened and how to keep it from happening again."

"That's what I wanted to warn you about before we go in."

"They, you know, the 'They' you hate, want you to figure out what happened so you can make sure it happens again."

"Allison, you know I don't do the whole cloak and dagger science."

"I know but since your last project was destroyed they feel like they deserve something for all the money they've spent."

"My project and my staff were nearly destroyed due to 'Their' inability to provide some basic security. So the question in my mind is who owes whom something?

"Catherine, this is why we're talking in the hall. You know how this works. Just work on it for a while and if you figure something out great, if you don't what can they do?"

"Fine and by the way, my project is still viable, but considering the breach in security I think it is for the best if no one other than the two of us know that."

"That is very good news. I will reallocate some funds and lab space under a different project name so you can finish it up in peace."

"Thanks, I won't need much, the hard part is done. Just lather rinse and repeat. You know the drill. Just give Kevin and I a couple of months and we will start using it here without anyone knowing."

"Speaking of Kevin, have you seen him yet?"

"Not yet. I figured I would pop in on him after you released your official statement."

"Yeah, thanks a lot for that. How am I supposed to spin this? One of the world's leading scientists, believed to have died in a tragic accident last week is feeling much better, in fact she would like to go for a walk?"

"Well you know 'there is a difference between mostly dead and all dead' to quote the Princes Bride."

"I suppose I could say you were dead, but you are feeling much better now or maybe that the rumors of your death are greatly exaggerated."

"See that's the spirit. If you have to eat humble pie you might as well have a little fun with it."

We were both giggling as we walked into the conference room. Around the very large table were people of great importance from every branch of the military and every government agency you have ever heard of and a few you haven't.

"Well I see the entire alphabet is accounted for." I whispered to Allison as we walked in.

"Good morning gentlemen. I hope you have all had time to look at the official accident investigation. I know there are some interesting findings and I'm sure you all have questions so, shall we get started?" Allison may as well have said release the hounds.

For the next three hours I was subjected to some very intense questioning. I was lying through my teeth to some of the most powerful people in the world. I kept telling myself "plausible deniability". There wasn't a person in this room that knew where I went and what happened so as long as my story was plausible there was nothing else they could do but believe me. The military men were giddy with the thought of invisibility until I made up a story about how everything was distorted and out of focus and that I had been unable to interact with anything or anyone. The spy boys wanted to know about access and how I traveled. Again they were disappointed that since I couldn't interact with anything. Walking was my only option and I had to wait to have other people open doors and press elevator buttons. By the time I was done I had convinced them that what had happened to me was in no way a good or useful thing. I did, however, agree to do a little research to see if I could recreate the circumstances that had caused this unfortunate accident. I felt pretty good about my story and everyone seemed to accept the fact that I hadn't died, I had been invisible for three days. On the other hand, I was stone walled completely on any explanation of who the men were who broke into my lab, how they gained access, and what had happened to them since. There was a lot of "above your pay grade", "need to know basis", "matter of national security" and other such nonsense floating around. I just needed them to assure me the security leak had been found and plugged. I really didn't need to know the details.

"So gentlemen before I go, I want to ensure that I have a full understanding of our current level of security. Since my accident you have apprehended ALL of the known and suspected parties involved in the attack on my lab? Is that correct?"

"Ms. Beaven your safety is our highest priority and we have done everything within our power to guarantee nothing like this can ever happen in the future."

"So let me make sure I understand that statement correctly. Since you didn't simply say 'yes', you still have someone in the wind don't you?" I demanded.

"Ms. Beaven I believe we have already established many of the details in this case are top secret and can not be discussed with you."

"Just as I suspected. You still don't have your mole. Thank you gentlemen I will see myself out. Or at least I'll try. Ms. Carter did the nice officer return my ID and phone?"

"Come with me and I'll make sure you get everything you need before you go."

"Thank you again gentlemen, good day."

I was doing my very best not to scream as I walked out of the conference room. There was more posturing that went on in that meeting than in a cage full of monkeys. I knew that was the way things worked but it never got any easier for me. The one important thing I learned was they still hadn't plugged their leak and until they did my work would have to be kept completely confidential. Allison had walked ahead of me to her assistant's office where she found my ID and my cell phone.

"Catherine, please be careful pushing these guys to hard."

"I did my best, but I really needed to know what sort of security concerns I should have and by evidence of what they couldn't and wouldn't say I have some big concerns."

"Just remember you have me and as far as I know you still have that handsome Major on your side."

"About that. I wouldn't exactly count on him. This whole dying thing sort of upset that apple cart. He is still on my side but I don't know how much longer he'll be at my side."

"Sorry to hear that, but you still have me and I'll do my best to keep you safe and under the radar."

"Thanks, now I really have to go find Kevin. Any idea where he may be hiding out?"

"Check Einstein's on Main Street I'm not sure he's left there since the day of the accident."

"Poor kid, I'll get him rebooted and raring to go in no time."

"Good luck Catherine and please, please be careful."

"Thanks for everything Alli and we'll do dinner at the ranch soon."

I knew as I walked out of the building I had just told some very important people including one of my best friends an entire pack of lies. I hated the fact that I couldn't tell the truth but for now I trusted no one, not Ali, not Major Allen and probably not Kevin but I still needed him.

Einstein's was a local brewpub frequented by many of the lab techs. It has 314 beers on tap and lots of other nerdy references. I found Kevin in the back under one of Jupiter's moons.

"Hey there stranger, how's it going?"

"I heard you were back from the dead, what's proper protocol for addressing you now? Ms. Undead, Madam Zombie or how about inconsiderate Biatch?

"Ouch that last one stung a bit. I suppose I earned it a little, but really Kevin you of all people know that I couldn't very well just walk into town and start chatting people up. I had to be debriefed. I reappeared at my Dad's house. He alerted Allison and I got a good night's sleep. Then I had to debrief Allison who reported to, well quite frankly everyone and I spent all day getting grilled like hamburger on the Fourth July until all I want to do is go to the ranch, lock the gate and not speak to anyone for a week. Instead I drag my sorry ass down here to snap you back to reality and what do I get? Would you like a beer Catherine, or I'm so happy you're not dead? No, I get inconsiderate Biatch. That's the best ya got?

"Fine would you like a beer Catherine you inconsiderate Biatch, that I am so happy is still alive and happier yet isn't a brain eating undead zombie."

"See with just a little effort you can do so much better."

"Do you really want a beer? I'll buy."

"Hell yes you will. So are we good?"

"Yeah we're good. You really did scare the hell out of us."

"So I've been told. I do have some questions about what happened, what it looked like, what it felt like from your perspective."

"They've got you working on doing it again don't they?"

"No, I convinced them that what happened to me is useless as a technology but I would really like to understand what happened so we don't accidentally do it again."

"Did they buy that? 'Cause I know you better than that."

"Yes they bought it and we will soon have a new home but mum's the word on that. I'm very serious, don't tell a soul and don't trust a soul. I really don't want an encore performance."

"Me neither."

"So what have you been working on during your period of mourning?"

"I started wondering how those guys knew so much about our lab and our security. I did my own little investigation and found that we had bugs. Lots of them."

"How is that possible with the electromagnetic field thingy?"

"You really are remedial when it comes to electronics aren't you?"

"Yes, we've been over this. Anyway, the bugs."

"The bugs were implanted in electronics that were designed to function inside the electromagnetic field and worked on our network. Things like our phones, our video feeds, our security system."

"They used our stuff to hack us?"

"Yes Ma'am, so you don't need to tell me not to trust anyone."

"Was your phone bugged?"

"Yes and I bet yours is too. They aren't the eaves dropping kind of bugs they are the access to all your data kind of bugs."

"Check my phone." I said tossing it across the table.

"Have you lost you mind? I can't do that here. Look around you Catherine."

"Then I guess I lost my LANL issued phone." I said as I dropped it on the floor, stomped on it and tossed it in the nearest trash.

"Catherine, I did miss your style. You just don't believe in overkill do you?"

"I've learned one thing this week. Life is unpredictable. No reason not to meet it head on. With that I need to get to the phone store before they close. I probably will not see you for a few days while I get things worked out. Since you have enlightened me to our electronic concerns I will go old school and just write you a note. If I can't find you I will leave it at the bar. Just check with them in a few days if you haven't heard from me."

"Sounds good boss, be careful. If you call I will know something is up, sort of our own personal 911."

"Okay, gotta go, now go outside and get a little sun, you look like hell."

"Love you too Catherine." Kevin shouted after me as I walked away.

The phone store was just a few doors down. I got myself a new phone and headed for the ranch. I had an idea but I had to fill Dad in before I tried anything. My new phone had to be charged so I would just have to go to his house without calling. Maybe I would be lucky enough to interrupt him for once.

Dad's car was in his driveway when I drove up.

"Good, the old man's home."

"I may be old but I not deaf." Dad said stepping out from behind the garage.

"Actually you are, but I see those hearing aids I bought you are working nicely."

"What are you doing in my neighborhood? You never stop by without calling first."

"I um, lost my phone, I stopped and picked up a new one but it has to charge. I thought I could charge it here before I headed back to the ranch."

"Sure kid, come on in."

"Dad, what's Charlie doing here? I thought we agreed you would take him to the ranch today so he could spend some time in his kennel."

"Well, I thought since this was your first day back to work it would probably be a long one, so I figured he could spend the day with me. We made you lasagna. I just put it in the oven so it would be done and waiting for you when you got home. I left you a voicemail but I guess you didn't get it."

"Thanks Dad. That was real sweet but how am I ever going to get him used to his kennel if he keeps spending his days with you?"

"I don't think he needs that silly kennel. He is a very good boy."

"Of course he is when he has constant entertainment. He needs to learn to be alone and that I will come back to get him."

"Maybe you should just charge your phone and do your important scientist stuff and leave Charlie and I alone."

"Okay Dad, thanks for the lasagna and thanks for letting me charge my phone. Since Charlie is here I'm in no hurry to get back to the ranch and I have something I need to talk to you about. Can we go out to your shop?"

"You hate my shop. You say you can't think in there because it is so disorganized. Why do you want to go to the shop?"

"I need to borrow a tool, come on lets go to the shop. You too Charlie, let's go."

Dad had a detached garage that he used as his workshop. I had put in cabinets and hung peg board over the years trying to help him keep some sort of organization but inevitably his tool box was empty, the work bench was covered, and the floor was a mine field of half completed projects. Dad was right, I hated his shop but I knew that it was set up with it's own utilities. At one time he thought he would rent it out as a studio or something. If someone was watching me they would be watching Dad too, but I seriously doubt if anyone would have bugged Dad's shop.

"Catherine what are we doing out here?"

"Dad, I think your house may be bugged. I have reason to believe there may be some people following me and one of the best ways to track me is to track you."

"Catherine, what's going on? You were acting very odd the day you disappeared and Major Allen had placed those guards at your gate. Now you are telling me you think my house is bugged. What are you working on and why are people trying to hurt you?"

"Dad I didn't say anyone was trying to hurt me just follow me."

"I know I'm not supposed to know anything and I don't have security clearance but a few of your lab techs stopped by after your accident. They may have let slip that there was some sort of attack on your lab the day of your accident."

"Dad, stop right there. I can't talk about anything that happens or happened at my lab. It's for your safety. Now for my safety as we discussed I didn't tell Allison and company what really happened when I disappeared or anything about Charlie and his collar."

"You know your aren't making any sense. Why can't you tell me what's happened at the lab if you can tell me about Abe?"

"One thing has nothing to do with the other. Whoever is following me is after my energy project. The last thing in the world I want them to do is stumble upon Charlie's collar. They won't know to ask you about Charlie, his collar or Abe so it is safe for you to help me with that. If they think you know anything about my other work, if you let slip any minor detail about what I do then you may be in danger. Does that make any sense?"

"A little, but you're not the cloak and dagger kind. You said so yourself, so why aren't you letting Major Allen handle all of this so you can do what you do best like figuring things out? Things like Charlie's collar?"

"Dad please understand right now you and Charlie are the only ones I can trust. No one can know what I'm doing here in your shop. Not Major Allen, not Allison, no one. I am vetting Kevin right now and if he is the man I think he is I will be able to trust him but until I'm sure, not even Kevin."

"Catherine did you hit your head?"

"Yes Dad, but I'm not impaired. Please trust me on this and just do as I ask. I really need your help."

"I wasn't questioning your sanity. You're bleeding."

I instinctively ran my hand over the wound on my head. I had nearly forgotten about it. I thought it was nearly healed. But as from the looks of the fresh red blood on my hand it was anything but healed. As I felt the wound I could tell it had gotten infected. It was hot and really tender.

"Damn it, how am I going to explain this? I said showing Dad the blood on my hand.

"Let's get you in the house and get it cleaned up to see what needs to be done."

"Fine just remember not a word of any of this leaves this shop."

Just as we walked around the house Major Allen pulled into the drive.

"Hey I've been looking all over for you. Your phone is going straight to voicemail and no one has seen you in hours. What happened? You're bleeding, who did this? What happened Catherine did they come after you again?"

"Whoa, easy big fella, you need to stop talking and start thinking." I said in my sternest cowgirl voice pitching a sideways glance at my Father.

"Can we just get inside to get a look at your head and maybe stop the bleeding?" Dad insisted.

134

"Thanks Dad, can you get me a towel, some hydrogen peroxide, some Q-tips and a pair of tweezers?"

"Yeah, I'll bring the first aid kit too, who knows what else you may need. Major Allen, get a chair and set it on some newspapers in the middle of the kitchen floor, right under the light so we can get a good look at this and she won't bleed all over my floor."

"The love and concern is overwhelming Dad." I yelled after him as he went to get all the first aid stuff.

"Catherine, what happened?" Major Allen asked in a much calmer voice.

"Dad and I were out in the shop and one of his projects toppled over whacking me on the head. I'm sure it's nothing; you know how easily your head bleeds. Now why the full-blown panic attack in the driveway? That's very unlike you. I think you may have frightened Dad."

"Sorry, I don't know what came over me. I called you after the debriefing to see if you wanted to meet for lunch or something and you didn't call me back. I tried again and still no answer. I knew you weren't working on anything today and it seemed very odd for you to not at least text me back so I started looking around town for you. No one had seen you since you left Einstein's. So I put a trace on your phone. I found it in the trash at Einstein's smashed all to bits. My mind went to the worse case scenario. I called your Dad and when he didn't answer I came over here to find you bleeding in the driveway. I guess this has all been a little harder on me than I realized."

"Major Allen, you are a mere mortal. You were truly worried about me. I'll try not to let that get around it could ruin your tough guy image."

"A little compassion would be nice Catherine, remember I was supposed to bury you yesterday."

"I'm sorry and I'm sorry I didn't answer my phone. As you saw I dropped it at Einstein's and as I was getting off my bar stool to pick it up I tripped and stepped on it smashing it to bits. I went to the phone store and got myself another one and came here to charge it. See, it's sitting on the countertop right over there. Dad's been working on a new project so we went out to the shop. You know what a death trap that place is and it shouldn't come as a surprise after the day I've been having that I got whacked in the head. So if you can let Dad clean up my head I'll get my new phone activated and you can take me to lunch or whatever."

"As tempting as that is I have to get ready to go to Washington. That's what I was going to tell you over lunch. I have to meet with the joint chiefs tomorrow to go over the day of your disappearance. I will be in Washington through the weekend. I wanted to see if you would consider staying with your Dad while I was gone."

"Can I assume your meeting is to discuss the fact you still have a mole? I know you can't answer that but I spent all morning getting the run around and the one thing they wouldn't say was our security level is back to normal. So yes, I can stay with Dad for a few days. Maybe I'll help him organize that death trap of a shop out there."

"That's it? No argument, no I can handle this, no my work must go on, nothing, just yes. How hard did you hit your head?"

"I think it's a good idea. Allison is still working on getting me a new workspace. Kevin is rebooting and quite frankly I can't handle another run in like the last one. This is a good time to spend a little time with Dad and Charlie. You can be my excuse.

You know that'll make him feel good if he thinks he's helping you."

"Feel good about what?" Dad asked returning with the first aid kit.

"Major Allen wants me to stay here for a few days. Would that be okay?"

"Of course, you and Charlie can stay as long as you need."

"Thanks Dad, now can you clean up my head. Major Allen, I think it's time for you to go. I'll be fine. Text me if you need anything."

"I can tell when I'm no longer needed. Thank you Sir for taking such good care of her. If she gets out of line, give me a call I'll send in some backup."

"Thanks Major, I'll keep and eye on her for you."

With that the Major was gone and Dad started cleaning my head.

"Geez Dad, what are you doing mining for gold or cleaning out a wound?"

"You have something in here. This is why it got infected and opened back up."

"What is it?"

"I'm not sure, give me a minute. I'm going to get a cup to put it in once I get it out. When was your last tetanus shot?"

"It wasn't that long ago. Just dig whatever is in there out and douse it with Schreiners instead of hydrogen peroxide. That'll make sure it heals."

"You know that stuff is for horses right?"

"What I know is that it works, and my head won't bleed anymore."

"I've just about got it. It looks likes apiece of metal, maybe a small piece of brass? Hard to say I'll let you figure that out. Now hold on to your socks this is going to sting a bit," Dad warned me before he poured on the Schreiners.

"Holy shit! That stings on a fresh cut."

"You could probably use a stitch or two but I know there's no way that is going to happen."

"Thanks Dad, now let's go take a look around your shop."

Dad knew I was reluctant to talk in the house until I could have it swept for any kind of electronic surveillance devices. Once we were inside the shop I started going over my plan.

"Dad, you know I have to understand out how Charlie's collar works and I don't think I can work on it at the Lab. You may have been right, I shouldn't have gone back to work but I think I'll need the lab at some point to test some of my theories."

"What do you need me to do?"

"I need you to clean this shop up. Seriously, I need to be able to work in here without killing myself. I need the floor clean and clear. Do you still have that old typewriter?"

"Yes, I still have the typewriter. Why"

"I'm going to have to go old school, it's hard to electronically spy on things that aren't electronic. I don't suppose you have a new ribbon for it?"

"Yes as a matter of fact I do. I bought a box of them when the shop on Main Street closed. I figured they would get real hard to find a probably real expensive."

"I love you, you old pack rat."

"Catherine! What are you planning to do and why do I have a feeling I'm not going to like it?

"I'm going to use Charlie's collar again. This time intentionally. I need to conduct an experiment so I can understand how it works. I want you to keep a journal of exactly what happens using your old typewriter. Once you're done, burn the paper you typed on. Don't keep anything written down where it can be found. Make sure you put the typewriter back wherever you've been keeping it so no one would notice it has been used. I'll clean the floor up while you go get the typewriter. Make sure you put a new ribbon in it."

"Why am I burning the journal? What's the point of typing it and then destroying it?"

"Your typewriter ribbon will have a complete record of everything you typed. Just remember not to backspace neatness doesn't count. Once you're finished remove the new ribbon and put the old one back in. Keep the ribbon with your journal on it in the box with all the other ones. No one will ever find it if you hide it in plane sight."

"Are you planning on doing this now?"

"You saw how worried the Major was when he couldn't find me for a few hours. I won't be able to try this with him around. He'll be gone for three days. I should be able to run this experiment and be back before he get's back from Washington. I think I'll be able to go and come right back but I don't know."

"What about how worried I am?"

"Dad, you know what I'm doing and you know I can come back because I have. So don't worry I'll have lots more data to work with this time."

"You can't be serious, your head is still bleeding from the last time you used that collar and now you want to use it again before you have any idea how it works?"

"What did you do with that dress I was wearing when I got back?"

"Don't you change the subject, young lady! I think this is a very bad idea!"

"It probably is. Now get me that dress."

While Dad went to find my dress I cleaned up an area of the floor where I could stand. Then I removed Charlie's collar and reset the code to 3H2R11.

"That should get me back to Abe."

Just then Dad showed up with my dress.

"Fantastic, I have Charlie's collar set to return to Abe. I know where I'm going and who'll be there. Don't worry Dad I'll be fine. Can you hold Charlie's collar while I put on this dress?"

"I don't suppose there is any way to talk you out of this?"

"No." I shouted from the bathroom.

"Please be careful Catherine."

"I will. Now how do I look?"

"Ridiculous but I'm sure Abe will approve."

"I'll be back in a flash. If I don't come right back don't panic. The collar may require some recharge time, that's one of the things I need to know. It may take a day or two. I know it worked after three days so that would be the outside, if I'm not back in 72 hours call Kevin and Major Allen and let them know what I did. Now sit down at your old typewriter and record everything you see and hear when I do this."

"I love you and you better come back."

"I love you to Dad and I'll be back, I promise." I said as I started rubbing Charlie's collar.

Benjamin Beaven 2.0

"Okay, that was odd." I said looking at Dad

"Catherine where have you been and why are you dressed like that?" Dad questioned as he gave me a big hug.

"Okay let me rephrase. This is odd. Dad I never left and you are the one who found the dress for me." I said looking around.

Things weren't quite right. The shop was clean; the tools were all hung on the wall. Dad had changed shirts.

"Catherine you have been gone for a week and I certainly have never seen that dress before. What happened and why are you bleeding?"

"I hit my head a few days ago don't you remember. You pulled something out of it just a few hours ago."

Just then Charlie ran in.

"Hey Charlie it's good to see you boy."

"That's not Charlie, you had Charlie with you. That's Lucy. Where is Charlie anyway?"

"Lucy, who the hell is Lucy?"

"Lucy is Charlie's sister. Remember we picked them out of the same litter. You picked Charlie and I picked Lucy."

"Dad I think we both need to sit down. Please tell me you have a bottle of Bourbon out here."

"Catherine you know I do, you gave it to me. It's in that bottom drawer."

I reached in the bottom drawer and pulled out a bottle of Basil Hayden and two glasses. I poured some for each of us while Dad went and got the first aid kit. Dad returned with the first aid kit and started cleaning up my head again.

"Dad, just leave it! It should be clean. It'll stop bleeding soon. Just sit down and talk to me."

"Let me pour some of this herbal stuff on it."

"Thanks Dad, not now, please sit down and have a drink with me. What I'm going to tell you will sound crazy but I assure you it's not."

"Catherine, nothing you're going to tell me will sound crazy. What is crazy is that you don't remember Lucy, you are wearing a ridiculous dress that you seem to think I should remember and you don't remember we were working on this project together. When you didn't come back after 48 hours I thought something must have gone wrong then when you didn't come back for nearly a week. I was very worried you may never come back. Now you're back and I think this bump on the head has confused you."

"Dad, I'm not Catherine, or at least not your Catherine and you're not my Dad even though you look just like him."

"What do you mean you're not Catherine and I'm not your father?"

"I found Charlie and this collar about a week ago in the river near my ranch. I accidently activated it and transported myself to another dimension. I was beginning to understand what I had done when I then inadvertently transported myself back. Now I was attempting to transport myself back and I ended up here."

"You're not Catherine?"

"No."

"You found Charlie and his collar but you didn't find Catherine?"

"No. I'm sorry. Let me get this straight. Charlie is your Catherine's dog and she works for LANL?"

"Yes."

"The two of you developed this technology together?"

"Yes."

"Catherine used this device to transport herself and Charlie. She and Charlie were somehow separated. Now I have used Charlie's collar to transport here. Does that mean I have stranded Catherine in another dimension?"

"Possibly, Catherine should have her own transporter. The one you are using is actually for the dog."

"I didn't know, I didn't see her, I don't know what happened to her. I only found Charlie. Sir, I'm so very sorry."

"Is that the way you dress where you're from?"

"No sir. The first time I used this collar I ended up with Abraham Lincoln. I thought I was going back there when some how I ended up here. I was sure I had set the collar to the same code as before but for some reason I came here. Since you helped Catherine develop this technology maybe you can explain to me how it works."

"Do you think she is dead?"

"I don't know sir. Maybe, I hope not. When I went to Abe's I ended up in the river and I managed to get out alive. That's how I got the cut on my head. I was naked and cold when Abe found me but I was alive. Maybe the same thing happened to her."

"If Charlie's collar is a back up then Catherine should have her own correct?"

"Yes she has her own transporter. So why hasn't she used it?"

"Sir, maybe it's broken, maybe she lost hers in the river. There are lots of reasonable explanations. I'll go back and look for her. I'll find out what happened and I'll come back and tell you."

"You know you can't go back for 48 hours don't you?"

"No, actually I didn't know that. Would you mind if I stayed with you and Lucy for a couple of days?"

"If you promise you will help me find Catherine and bring her back here safe."

"I promise I'll do everything I can to find your Catherine and bring her back to you. I know my Dad would be going crazy if he hadn't seen me for a week. Thank you for letting me stay. By the way what should I call you?"

"Just call me Dad, that's fine with me."

"Thanks Dad. Now would you happen to have change of clothes here I could borrow?"

Dad and I headed into the house where things looked very similar but oddly different. Everything seemed slightly more modern. The furniture was different but it was the same color. The appliances in the kitchen looked newer and sleeker but the kitchen table was exactly the same. I mindlessly started wandering down the hall to what should have been my room. The decor was different but I liked it.

"That's not your room, that's your sister's room. Yours is the next one on the left." Dad said as he politely followed me.

"I, I mean Catherine, has a sister?"

"Yes, don't you have a sister?"

"No, I'm an only child. Where is she now?"

"She is off saving whales or some nonsense like that. She will be back for the holidays, then off again with that crazy boyfriend of hers."

"So, no grandkids?"

"None yet. I keep hoping you and that Major of yours will settle down and give me a few."

"Major?" I said quickly turning to face him.

"This is so odd having to explain Catherine's life to you. I feel like you should know but I don't know how you would. I think you'll find some jeans in the drawer and maybe a sweatshirt or two in the closet."

"Thanks I'll get changed and you can fill me in on Catherine's life over some more bourbon."

I had just slipped into some jeans and a Stanford sweatshirt when I heard a commotion in the kitchen.

"Dad, everything all right?"

"What the hell is going on here Mr. Beaven? You filed a missing person report, you've had me worried sick for the past three days. Now I get a hit on the DNA sensors and you try to tell me she isn't here. Well if it's not Catherine, then who the hell is she?" The Major turned to pointing at me.

I walked directly toward him never losing eye contact. I could see in his eyes behind all that blustering there was real fear. He cared for Catherine like Major Allen cared for me. As I stood toe to toe with him I finally spoke.

"Tom, is that you?"

"Yes, Catherine of course it's me, but why did you call me Tom?"

"Glad to see some things don't change."

"Catherine what are you talking about, where have you been and why was your Father lying to me about you being here."

"Dad, get the Bourbon. We're going to be here a while."

"I don't need a drink, I need an explanation." The Major demanded.

"How about both? Just have a seat and Dad and I will be right back to answer all of your questions."

I sat the Major down on the sofa and went in the kitchen to help Dad with the drinks.

"How much does he know about the collar gizmo?" I quietly asked Dad.

"Nothing, this was strictly off the record, something we were working on together."

"Okay, follow my lead. I'll do my best to protect all of us."

Dad and I headed out to the sofa where a very angry Major was sitting.

"First let me start with I'm sorry. Dad should've never tried to hide me from you. Bad Dad." I said smiling at Dad.

"You think this is a joking matter Catherine, you think you and your Dad can just placate me with good Bourbon, a few one liners and I'll forgive you. Not this time." The Major said while rattling his ice cubes.

"Easy there big fella. I'm not making light of anything or trying to placate you I am sincere in my regret that this situation has caused you so much trauma. The first thing you are going to have to understand is Dad was not lying. Catherine, the Catherine you know is not here. I am not her, she is not me, and we are not one in the same. Now stop rattling those ice cubes and drink your Bourbon."

"What do you mean? You are too Catherine. If you weren't you would not have set off the DNA sensors."

"I have the same DNA as Catherine? Well I guess I would since we have the same parents. What I'm trying to say is that your Catherine and I are the same person from two separate dimensions. I was working on an experiment in my lab at my LANL and I accidentally swapped places with her. I will swap back as soon as I can and you'll have your Catherine back and I'll be back where I belong. Understand?"

"No Catherine, I don't understand but that's something I'm all too used to."

"It'll only take another 48 hours plus or minus before everything will be back as it should be. Until then, please keep this strictly between us. If your LANL is like my LANL they'll do anything to get their hands on a new technology, even if that means stranding your Catherine in my dimension. I feel really bad that this has happened to her and I want to set it straight as soon as possible."

"So let me get this straight, you look like Catherine, you share the same DNA as Catherine, you are here with Catherine's Father but you are not Catherine."

"Major, I promise you this is not my daughter. I wish she were, then I would have her home safe and sound but she is not. Now please listen to her and help her get Catherine back. You aren't the only man who loves her you know." Dad said wiping away a tear.

With that he left the Major and I alone on the sofa to work things out.

"Okay, I'll have to make up some story as to why the DNA sensors went off. I think I can only keep this quiet for a few days. Anything more and someone will get wind of this, then there is nothing I can do to help either of you."

"Do you love her?"

"That's a very personal question to ask."

"Sorry, it's just odd talking to you this way."

"You and I, we, really? In another world?"

"Yes, we are, well, we have, yeah things seem the same in the other dimension. We are from the same world just different dimensions."

"That is very odd. How can we be from the same world? Did you travel through time?"

"No, It's 2011 in my dimension too. Just 2011 in my dimension is a little different than here."

"This isn't making any sense. How do I know you aren't making all this up."

I reach over and stuck my hand inside the Major jacket. I pulled out a small black velvet bag tied with a red satin ribbon.

"Hey, how did you know that was in there? Does Catherine know about this?"

"I don't know. It was just a hunch for me for a long time. I've never seen what's inside. May I?"

"Wait, you are telling me that in another dimension there is a guy like me who is in love with you who carries around and engagement ring and has never asked you to marry him?"

"Yes, do you believe me now? Who else knows about that ring? I'm guessing no one."

"Your Dad knows."

"You asked my Father if you could marry me before you asked me. You know it's been a long time since you had to declare women as property on your taxes and have you heard we got the right to vote? Why don't you take your club and your ring back to the cave you crawled out of your Neanderthal?"

"Wait just a minute. I didn't ask your Father anything I asked Catherine's and I think she would think that was a respectful and traditional thing to do. I hope she wouldn't think of it as passing ownership of her. Oh god, that's exactly how she would view that isn't it? Well you're not Catherine so I can still fix this right? Would you like to see the ring?

I carefully untied the ribbon and poured the contents into the palm of my hand. It was beautiful. A wide titanium band engraved with a Celtic knot, with a single emerald cut ruby set in the center. Engraved inside the band was "Carpe Diem".

"It is perfect. She will love it."

"Will you put it on to see if it fits?"

"No, That ring is not for me. She should be the first to wear it."

"Yeah you're probably right. I've just been waiting a long time to see it on someone's hand."

"When she gets back, why don't you take it out of your pocket and see what happens? Just don't mention her Dad and I think everything will work out just fine."

"Maybe I'll try that."

"Do or do not there is no try."

"You have Yoda too?"

"We're not barbarians, of course we have Yoda."

"Well it's nice to see that our worlds, I mean dimensions aren't that different. So how are you going to get back to your Major and are you going to accept his proposal?"

"I told you I don't know what's in that little bag in his pocket and he's never proposed. I'm going to do some work with Catherine's father tomorrow and hopefully I can create a way to get back. As soon as I'm back I can send Catherine home. I promise I'll do everything in my power to get her back here as quickly as possible."

"When you swapped places is there any chance Catherine could have been hurt."

"Unfortunately, yes. I don't know what happened when we switched places but it is possible that either of us could have been injured. I got a nasty bump on the head so hopefully nothing worse happened to her."

"Does this swap have anything to do with the two of you having the same DNA?"

"Possibly, these are all things I will be working on over the next few days. I know this may sound odd, but could we just order in some Chinese and spend a nice quiet evening pretending everything is normal? I've had a real rough week, I'm tired and more than a little fragile. I really need to just stop moving and stop thinking for a few hours. Could we do that?"

"Promise never to call me a Neanderthal again?"

"Promise. Is caveman of limits too?"

"Yes, I'll check on your Dad, make a call to the office, then get the Chinese. What would you like?"

"Surprise me. I bet you know what my favorite is."

Some Things Never Change

The Chinese food was great, Major Allen knew exactly what I liked. Dad went to bed right after dinner. I think the whole thing was just too stressful for him. Major Allen and I sat on the sofa and compared stories about our respective lives. I learned that he secretly hated the fact I always had my iPod on shuffle.

"Why can't you listen to an album the way the artist made it? They take great pride in the way they organize their songs and you never listen to them in order."

"Wow, obsess much? Why can't you ever wear anything that doesn't look like a uniform?"

"Why don't you ever iron anything"?

"Why do you pay to have your jeans pressed and starched?

"Okay, I see we share our differences. Have you ever asked your Major Allen any of those questions?'

"Hell no, what about you?"

"Not a chance, why fight about stuff that in the end doesn't really matter?"

"Aha, something we agree on. What about secrets?"

"What about them?"

"Come on I know there are things you haven't told her. Now's your chance, it's like confession. I can't disclose anything you tell me. It wouldn't be ethical."

"I'm not ratting out my other self. Man that sounds odd."

"I know. There's no reason to believe you would be keeping the same secret. Tell me something embarrassing or annoying. If you're keeping a big secret please keep it, I don't want to know."

"I have a thing for cocktail waitresses. If you really want to get me going, get one of those outfits that they wear in Vegas."

"That's not a secret a blind woman can see how you look at a cocktail waitress."

"If you know that, why haven't you ever dressed up like one?"

"I don't like objectifying women. It's bad enough that you do it, I'm not going to encourage you."

"Not even on my birthday?"

"You are such a boy. I'll keep it in mind. Now tell me something I don't know."

"I'm highly allergic to quinine."

"Quinine, who uses quinine anymore? What happens if you take quinine and why would you keep that a secret?"

"No one uses quinine anymore which is why I never mention it. It makes me really ill but it won't actually kill me, so the military thinks it's safer for people not to know. I'm at a much greater risk of being intentionally poisoned than accidentally dosed."

"Well that's interesting. I have no idea if my Major Allen is allergic to quinine. I'll have to ask."

"I hate the way you kiss when you get passionate."

"Ouch! That's not very nice."

"I'm sorry, but I'm sure she won't tell you and things would work out better for you if you dialed it back a couple of notches. Kissing isn't a competitive sport."

"I think I'm being falsely accused. There is no evidence to support the fact that I am anything but a quality kisser."

"What, you want a quality control check?"

"For purely scientific reasons I assure you."

"That's what you say to all the cocktail waitresses isn't it?"

"Hey, that was a cheap shot."

"Did you really think I wouldn't use your confession against you?"

"No, but I did think it would take longer."

"I think you should go, I need to get some sleep. If you would like to see your Catherine anytime in the near future I need to get to work first thing in the morning."

"I'll be back tomorrow afternoon. If you need anything from the lab have your dad call me. I'm leaving now, this is your last chance for that kiss."

"Go home Major Allen you will have to wait for your Catherine to come home for a real kiss." I said kissing him on the check and shoving him out the door.

I slept well that night. Major Allen's playful flirtatiousness had made me remember all the things I really liked about him and why we had stayed together so long. I dreamed about our first date, our first camping trip and that disastrous trip we took to New Orleans. I awoke to the familiar smell of bacon and eggs.

"There better be coffee to go with that." I said entering the kitchen and kissing Dad on the check.

"Coffee's in the pot and there's cream in the fridge if you want it."

"No, I take my coffee black."

"Finally something you and Catherine do different."

"She takes her coffee with cream?"

"No she thinks it's an abomination to add anything to coffee."

"She would have said, 'I take mine like God intended not like you pansies drink it'."

"I was trying to be polite. I'll do better next time."

"Eat your breakfast, we have lots of work to do and not a lot more time. I figure first thing tomorrow morning you will be able to go back and start looking for Catherine."

"I know my dad will be happy to see me tomorrow and I'm sure he'll do everything he can to help me find your Catherine."

"No matter what happens, do you promise you will come back and let me know? I can't bear the thought of losing her but knowing would be so much better than always wondering."

"I promise, I'll find her no matter what happened and I will get her back to you."

Dad and I worked all day building a new transporter. I wanted to understand how this technology worked so if I needed to rebuild one to get Catherine home I could. I was very impressed with the fail-safes Catherine and her father had built in. Charlie's collar was actually a redundancy. If Catherine's transponder were to fail she would have Charlie's to make sure she could always get home. The transporters were devised so only Catherine and Ben's DNA could activate them. Neither of them had considered in each dimension there was the potential for someone else to have identical DNA.

"Dad, let me get this straight. If the transporter is set to a dimension other than this one and it is activated and not reset it will automatically return here?"

"Yes, it is a fail safe, if one of us were to be injured or lose consciousness the transporter would automatically return us home as soon as it regained charge."

"That's pretty smart so what happened for me to end up here? I had it set for the same dimension I had accidentally visited. Why did it return me here?"

"You set it and activated it right away?"

"No, I changed into that dress. Dad held it for me while I changed."

"So I, Dad, whatever, touched it after you set it?"

"Yes, which means he activated it with his DNA and since I didn't reset it, TA-DA here I am."

"One mystery solved. But now I'm more concerned Catherine should've come home by now."

"Yeah I know. Her transporter is either broken, lost or she is…"

"It must just be broken and since I have her back up, it will take her some time to get it working. Our technology isn't as advanced as yours. The most benign explanation is usually true, right?"

"I think you may be sweeter than my Catherine."

"Oh please don't let anyone hear you say that. It would ruin my reputation."

"So if we get another transporter working can we set the fail safe to my dimension?"

"Sure, that would probably be a good idea, since we should be the only people in any dimension who know how this works we probably want to keep tabs on one another."

"What have you and Catherine done to ensure this technology doesn't fall into the wrong hands?"

"We only have two transporters and they are coded to our DNA. We have destroyed all of our research and if you tamper with one of the transporters it will self-destruct. If we're lucky we will get another one to work but only because everything is fresh in my mind. I promise you in another six months, not even Catherine will be able to do this again without starting from scratch."

"How long did it take to build the first one?"

"Twenty five years."

"Someone would have to be very committed to wait that long for another one."

"How many different dimensions have you traveled to?

"None, this was our maiden voyage. You've used this thing more than anyone."

"That's a little scary. So you don't know if there are any side effects to this?"

"Nope, we've calculated that there shouldn't be but honestly there is no way to know."

"I guess that's another reason to keep tabs on one another."

"When I went to the dimension where I met Abraham Lincoln, he had a dog just like Charlie. His name was even Charlie. When I found Charlie in the river, I named him Charlie before I found his collar. How does Charlie fit into all of this?"

"I have no idea. Catherine came in with Lucy and Charlie a few weeks ago. They are littermates and they are about three months old now. As far as I know Charlie shouldn't have anything to do with this technology."

"You do know, that the code for your dimension is 'CHAR1E' don't you."

"No it's not, it's 3H1r15."

"Which if you change the numbers to letters is 'CHAR1E'."

"I'd never made that connection. How on earth did you figure that out?"

"I have to guess if you didn't program it then Catherine did and if it made sense to her, it makes sense to me. Could she have withheld some piece of information? Maybe she thought it would keep you safe if you didn't know?"

"I suppose. It would be like her to do something like that. Unfortunately that means we may never get this transporter to work."

"If we can't get it to work, will one transporter work for both of us?"

"Transport you both simultaneously?"

"Yeah."

"Maybe since you share DNA. I think it might. If it doesn't work though I don't know what would happen to one or both of you."

"What could happen?"

"Lot's of very bad stuff or nothing at all."

"So, what I'm hearing is we really need to get this transporter to work or find Catherine so she can help me get this transporter to work."

"Find Catherine seems to be the answer of the day."

"First thing in the morning I will zap myself back to my fathers shop and find Catherine. Simple enough right?"

"Simple as can be."

"I think we've done everything we can do for today. Take the new transporter back to your dimension and Catherine can calibrate the fail safe to your dimension when you find her."

Dad and I headed back to the house. He seemed a little more optimistic than he had earlier. I really wanted everything to work out for the best. I didn't think I could bear to come back and tell him Catherine had drowned. Major Allen came by with pizza, beer and a bad B movie. Snuggled up on the sofa between Dad and Major Allen, I almost felt at home.

I woke up the next morning still on the sofa. Lucy was curled up behind my knees and someone had covered me with a blanket. Dad wasn't up yet and Major Allen must have gone home. Lucy and I headed into the kitchen to start the coffee. Dad had set the automatic timer on the coffee and it was just starting to brew.

"Wow, look at that Lucy. Catherine's dad can set the coffee pot. I wish my dad could master that."

"I haven't really figured it out. Catherine has it set so if I remember to add the coffee at night I will work. Otherwise it just makes a pot of hot water."

"For some reason that's very reassuring to me."

"What's wrong? Are you afraid you won't be smarter than both your Dads?"

"You have definitely raised the bar but I think I can manage." I said with a wink

"Do you want breakfast before you go?"

"Maybe a little, I think it's still a little early to head back. I also want to see if we can integrate a locator into our new transporter. Sort of an inter-dimensional peep or a transporter transponder."

"That's actually a great idea, why didn't we think of that before?"

"You hadn't lost one before. Necessity is the mother of invention."

Dad and I ate a quick breakfast and headed out to the shop. After a few hours we had devised a very simple locator device that we simply attached to the strap of the new transporter. Like the transporter itself, my DNA activated it.

"It's not pretty but I think it'll work. This will let me track you from here. It won't let us communicate but it will let me know you are alive and where to look for you if I need to. Before you use that transporter make sure Catherine checks it out thoroughly. I thought a lot about the whole Charlie connection last night and I'm sure Catherine must have kept something from me."

"I don't know if it was intentional or accidental but somehow Charlie's DNA is coded into this also. Catherine and I will sort it all out when I find her. I guess that means it's time to go. You know it'll be a few days before I can get her back but I will get her back to you I promise."

"I know you will, just make sure not to get yourself in a pickle helping her."

"What could be safer than the two of us working together?"

"I think the question is 'is anything safe with the two of you working together?"

"One last question. Has anyone ever tried to steal or sabotage one of Catherine's projects?"

"Oh yeah, there was a big hullaballoo last year. I don't know exactly what happened because it was 'Classified' but some armed men took over her lab for short time until her assistant and Major Allen outsmarted and out muscled them."

"Do you know who was behind the attack?"

"No, there was a pretty big shake up of desk jockeys after that and Catherine never said which one of them was ultimately responsible."

"Was Catherine close to any of the ones that left?"

"Catherine isn't close to any of them, you should know that, but I think she did like the deputy director, Allison Carter. I was real surprised to see her go and I really don't know if the two things were connected or just coincidental timing."

"I don't believe in coincidence."

"Neither does Catherine."

"Thanks dad, I'm going to go and find Catherine now."

"Godspeed, child, Godspeed."

With that I activated the transporter and faded away.

A Pure and Noble Soul

The walk to the temple was much harder than I'd imagined. Not only was I wearing twenty pounds of silk but also the dress was cut so straight I couldn't make a full stride. This became even more troublesome when we began climbing the steps. With the help of Heinrich and Peter I managed to drag myself to the massive wooden doors of the temple. A guard bowed politely and allowed us to pass into the courtyard. On the opposite side of the courtyard was a large bell next to a small pool of water sitting at the base of yet another set of steps. Waiting for us at the top of those steps were five Monks in red robes with golden sashes. As we reached the monks I hesitated for just a moment and turned to watch the sunset reflecting in the small pool. With my heart and mind filled with the awesomeness and beauty that surrounded the temple I was ready to meet the Dali Lama.

Inside the temple the air hung heavy with the smell of incense and the low hum of chanting monks. The monks directed us to a small area to remove our shoes. I quickly slipped out of my boots and gently rubbed my sock feet across the wooden floors. Centuries of sock feet had polished the wooden floors until they were as smooth and soft as the silk I was wearing. The monks led the way followed by Heinrich, Peter and then me. I wasn't sure if they would even allow a woman completely inside the temple so I trailed behind. As we walked I admired the architecture of the temple. The artistry and craftsmanship was a tribute to the people who not only managed to live in this inhospitable climate but they managed to thrive. Much of the work would have taken decades to complete. I could only imagine the amount of time and work that went into creating such a magnificent building. As we neared the Dali Lama's room the monks began to talk amongst themselves and look cautiously in my direction. I was fairly certain they were uncomfortable with me being allowed through the front gates now I was approaching their supreme leader and this was creating some strife. As the final set of doors opened I could see the young boy sitting on a throne of pillows surrounded by monks. Sitting behind him off to his right was a single woman. She looked unhappy, she did not look like she was a slave or a servant but she didn't look like she belonged either. She was an observer. For some reason she was allowed in but not accepted. Seeing her gave me hope that maybe I would be allowed into the inner sanctum. My hopes were soon dashed as two young monks stepped in front of me. I had reached the end of my journey and for now that was okay. I was allowed to sit on a beautifully carved bench and wait. As I sat on the bench I drifted into a dream. In my dream I was riding my appaloosa mare bare back through the bosque rounding up the herd. She had pushed them all together and then she began to run, as she ran they all began to follow once they were all following she broke into a full gallop with the entire herd thundering toward the barn behind her. I was merely a passenger; I sat close on her shoulders with her mane interlaced in my fingers. I leaned forward over her neck, closed my eyes and felt the world pass under her feet. My heart rate matched hers; her breath was mine and for a few minutes we were one creature. As we entered the paddocks she slowed just enough to let me slip off the side of her neck and place my feet on the ground. With that we were separate once more, she led the herd the rest of the way in at a polite trot while I closed the gates behind them. By the time I reached the barn everyone was getting a drink, except they were not drinking out of a trough they were drinking out of the small pool in the courtyard of the temple. As I approached the pool I could see the reflection of the temple and the sunset just as I had seen from the top of the steps. Just then I was awakened by one of the monks who had decided to take a seat on the bench beside me.

"Your horse is a beautiful creature and her soul is strong and pure." He said in perfect English never making eye contact with me.

"How could you possibly know I have a horse and that she has a strong soul?"

"Your thoughts were just with her and she with you. Very few people share thoughts with animals. It is a very good thing we believe."

"I was dreaming how could you know what I was dreaming about?"

"Thoughts are the only thing that we can know. Everything else is just perception. You know this; you showed her our temple in the water. Before you came into the temple you connected with everything you believe and feel. The men did not do that, they do not understand. You know these things but you do not fully understand them. Follow your horse, she is a good guide she will lead you just as she leads her herd."

Then the monk got up and walked away. Leaving me sitting on the ornate bench all alone. I wasn't exactly sure what had just happened but I felt very peaceful after my visit with the monk. I began thinking maybe there was more to this dimensional travel than I had realized. Maybe this was what the monks have been doing for centuries. I was starting to believe that it wasn't just Charlie's collar that had brought me here; maybe I wasn't the only one who could change dimensions. After a few moments Heinrich and Peter emerged. Followed by the five monks and the Dali Lama and the woman that had been seated behind him.

Heinrich spoke first.

"On behalf of the Dali Lama I would like to inform you that your transgressions have been forgiven and you will not be banished from Lhasa. I would also like to tell you that his mother has requested your presence at tea tomorrow."

"Thank you, I'm very happy to know I can stay in Lhasa and I'll be honored to have tea with the Mother of such an important young man."

"We have been contracted to do some tutoring for the Dali Lama as well as a small construction project. This will require us to spend a great deal of time at the temple. The Dali Lama has been generous enough to offer us a small cottage inside the temple walls. If you would like, you may stay there tonight while Heinrich and I prepare the things we will need for our new employment."

Peter seemed very pleased. The seamstress would have to be impressed now. The monk that had sat beside me on the bench escorted me to the cottage, while the other monks escorted Heinrich and Peter out of the temple. When we arrived at the cottage Charlie was sitting by the door.

"Charlie, how on earth did you get here?"

"He would not leave the temple gates. After I met you, I knew that this animal must be connected to someone who shared their thoughts with animals. I let him through the gates and asked him to wait. I told him I would bring you to him. He has a very old soul and a kind heart."

"Thank you for your kindness, Charlie is a very special dog. Would it be appropriate for him to come inside the cottage?"

"Charlie may accompany you anywhere you are allowed. You are connected and everyone here will recognize that."

"Would you please come in and talk with me? I would like to understand more about how you could see my dreams and how you know Charlie and I are connected."

"I can not. I am not your teacher. Go inside and rest. Let your mind find what it is looking for. You are a very powerful person if you do not use force."

"Could you at least tell me your name?"

"In this life I am called, Adoy."

With that the monk quietly left Charlie and I standing at the door of our cottage. Charlie and I went inside to find more of the same architecture I had been admiring in the temple. All of the furnishings were had carved with ornate filigree work. Someone had built a fire and there was a kettle hanging over it. A tea service was placed neatly on the hearth. On the bed folded and tied with a ribbon was a silk nightgown and a plush woolen robe. I was elated at the thought of getting out of this dress. The seamstress had done a fine job and it fit me perfectly but the design was for modesty and binding not for comfort. I managed to get myself unwrapped from my silk cocoon and into my nightgown and robe just as the kettle started to whistle.

"Charlie there are few things finer than properly enjoying a cup of tea."

I said looking into his expectant eyes. Charlie knew where there was tea there were biscuits and I had incapable of ignoring his soft brown eyes when he pleaded for a biscuit.

"All right just one but then we have to find us both something proper for dinner."

As Charlie and I sat enjoying our tea and biscuits there was a knock at the door. Without waiting for me to answer a young boy from the monastery came in with a tray of food. He placed a small bowl on the floor in front of the fire for Charlie and left everything else on the small table by the window for me. He never spoke a word and never made eye contact he was in and out before I could gather myself.

"Well look at this Charlie, they have delivery at the temple. Isn't that nice?"

Charlie and I enjoyed our dinner and then curled up together in our very soft bed. My mind kept going back to what the monk had said about being powerful without force. Power versus force is a concept often studied when you are dealing with non-linear dynamics, particle physics and chaos theory. Some of the new age spiritualists have concluded that this theory can be applied to our personal lives to help us reach our highest level of enlightenment. I have found a lot of the work I do with horses fits nicely into the simplest version of this theory. When your dealing with a 1000 pounds of aggravated animal it's nice to be able to use their energy to change the situation not yours. Subtle changes in behavior change pulling into leading and fear into cooperation. I thought I understood the principle of what he was suggesting but what did the monk mean by let my mind find what you are looking for? I don't think even my mind can find out how he
170

knew my dreams without some serious guidance and input. As I drifted of to sleep curled up with Charlie I was sure somehow this was the missing piece of my research. I only needed to figure out what the monk suggesting.

The following morning was crisp and cold. One of the young boys from the monastery came in early and revived my fire and set out a fresh tea service. Charlie and I pretended not to see him but as soon as he was gone Charlie gave me quick lick and headed for the bowl of yak milk he had left on the floor in front of the fire.

Before I managed to get out of bed and enjoy my tea there was a knock at the door and Heinrich and Peter walked in.

"Good morning boys. Would you like some tea?" I asked while putting on my robe.

"We would love some tea." Heinrich said in his overly exuberant way.

"Peter, how about you?"

"Yes, please. We can leave until you are properly dressed if you would like."

"Peter, you're very kind to offer but I'm in no hurry to get back in that dress."

"So one day you are an enemy of the state and the next they are bringing you breakfast in bed. It's quite a life you lead Catherine." Heinrich said pouring us all some tea.

"Yes and thank you both for whatever you told them to keep them from banishing me from Lhasa."

"Oh it wasn't what Peter and I said it was the mother of the Dali Lama. She made it very clear to all the monks and advisors that you were not to be harmed in any way. She said you had been in her dreams and you were very important to her and her son."

"Well that's good news. Things always work out better when I'm important. Peter will you be accompanying me to tea this afternoon? I will need and interpreter."

"I will interpret for you Catherine, if they will allow me. Contact with the Dali Lama's mother is highly discouraged and very restricted. It's hard to promote his divinity with his mother in the room. Since we will be working for him they may not want me to have any contact with her."

"No wonder she looks so unhappy. Her child is God incarnate and she was just the delivery person. That's got to sting a bit. Any idea what she wants to talk to me about or why she thinks I'm important to her son?"

"If possible, she makes less sense than you." Heinrich said in his teasing voice.

After Heinrich and Peter had finished their tea it was time for them to go. As much as I hated it I really needed to get dressed.

"All right this has been fun and informative. Now I need to get dressed and talk to a monk about a horse, then have a little tea party. After that I will probably be leaving, so if I don't see you again, it has been a pleasure to get to know both of you. I wish you both a long and happy life and please take good care of Charlie. He is a very special dog."

"Where do you think you are going this time of year? There is no way out of Lhasa right now." Heinrich protested.

"Heinrich, Peter, please do not worry and do not look for me. I have the ability to leave here without any harm coming to me. You have both been very kind and generous to me and I will always remember you. Now please go. If I can, I will say goodbye before I leave."

Both of the men looked very confused as I escorted them to the door. With a tremendous amount of effort I managed to get myself dressed then Charlie and I headed out to find our favorite monk.

In the courtyard next to the bell and the pool were three monks. They appeared to be praying as Charlie and I approached two of them stood and walked off while the other stayed. Head bowed in prayer. I stood quietly by the pool looking at the monk's reflection. The wind was causing small ripples in the pond giving the monks reflection the look of a mirage. As I stared into the pool I noticed a figure standing behind the monk in the reflection. As I focused on the figure I realized it was the reflection of my horse. The one I had been riding in my dream. I looked over at the monk who was still praying and I looked all around the courtyard, there was no horse. However, clearly reflected in the pool was my horse.

"Hey, stop that, leave her alone." I demanded of the praying monk.

"You came to me for answers, I have shown you how powerful your thoughts can be. Why are you angry?"

As the monk raised his head to speak I realized it was Adoy. I had come to find him and hopefully some answers but I was not prepared for what I was seeing.

"She is connected to me, you have brought her here and now she is looking for me. Don't you think that might confuse her?"

"Tell her you are here. Bring her from the pool to the courtyard. You brought yourself here, now bring her."

"It doesn't work like that."

"Anything you can do with technology you can do with your mind. It was your mind that made the technology, you have created the thought use it to bring her here."

I focused on the reflection in the pool. It was becoming more defined. I thought about what I knew about Charlie's collar and how it worked. As I thought the reflection became more distorted. Then I cleared my mind except for the memory of our last bareback ride. I closed my eyes, slowed my breathing, brought my heart rate down and felt her warm body between my knees. I could feel her heart beating in time with mine. I could feel the wind in my hair and I could hear Charlie barking. I opened my eyes to see why Charlie was barking. Across the courtyard the gates of the temple opened and in trotted a lone horse. A magnificent spotted horse. She trotted right up to me and put her head down to my feet. I lay across her neck and she lifted me onto her back. I felt the seams on my dress give way as I straddled her warm back. She trotted around the entire courtyard ensuring everyone had seen us then returned to the monk. I slipped off her back and placed my forehead to hers.

"Thank you. You are a pure and noble soul." I told her.

"I am sorry for any stress I caused you. Please return with peace and happiness." Adoy took his golden sash and wrapped it around her neck and led her to the pool. She nuzzled me and then walked into the pool. Disappearing back into her reflection. Soon her reflection was gone.

"What just happened?" I demanded.

174

"You manifested your horse and I sent her back. When you return you will find she is still wearing my sash."

"I didn't do that alone."

"Few things are done alone. But remember what one man can do, so can another. I have spent years learning to connect with others. You have a gift, a talent. If you choose to develop it you will be capable of great things. If you don't you will always need to rely on the technology you have created."

"Can the Dali Lama do that?"

"In every lifetime he learns how. That is how he continues to be reincarnated here and continues to raise his level of enlightenment."

"I would really enjoy spending some more time with you but I must meet the Dali Lama's mother for tea. I don't suppose you can manifest me up a new dress since I have ripped the seams out of this one?"

"Fabric repair is not something I have studied but I will send someone to your cottage with a new dress for you to wear to tea."

"Thank you. Thank you for everything. I think I may be beginning to understand something that people around here have known for centuries."

"I will not see you again before you leave. Be safe in your travels and remember you can return whenever you want. Focus on your thoughts and they will manifest."

I headed back to the cottage to get cleaned up for tea. I could smell the horse sweat on my clothes and hands and I had a small piece of mane hair intertwined between my fingers. I carefully took Charlie's collar out of my pocket and wrapped the horsehair around it. I needed something to anchor me to this place and this moment. I believed what the monk said, but I also knew that saying and doing are two very different things and what had just happened took a lot of energy from somewhere and I didn't know if I could ever manage to focus that much energy again.

Within moments there was a knock at the door and two young women arrived carrying a new dress and seeming very certain they were going to put me in it. I tried to protest but with amazing efficiency they stripped me of my current dress and redressed me in another beautiful garment of silk. Like the other dress it was one part kimono and one part Victorian era formal wear. Instead of a corset there was a silk wrap the was tied in a figure eight around your waist and across your shoulders; then your blouse, then the dress, then you were wrapped in an obi type sash which hung like an apron in the front. This outfit was complete with the traditional leg wraps and the toed socks which made me look like I had cloven hooves for feet. After I was dressed they began working on my hair. They braided ribbons of silk into my hair and then placed a square hat on top of my head. I thought I looked very silly but they were quite impressed with my new outfit. As they applied their finishing touches, the gaggle of five monks arrived at the cottage to escort me to tea.

"Good afternoon, thank you for joining me." The Dali Lama's mother said in English.

"Good afternoon to you also, Ma'am. I am pleased to find that you speak English."

"I learned it just for this day."

"Really? How did you know you would need to speak English so long ago?"

"When I was a young girl I had a dream that I would be the mother of the next Dali Lama. In my dream I learned that this incarnation of the Dali Lama would be different from the previous thirteen. This Dali Lama would have to go out into the world and teach all the people of the world about our way of life. We could no longer stay hidden in our sacred city. In my dream you came to the temple and introduced the Dali Lama to good men from the outside world who would teach him and help him. I have waited many years for you to arrive. I knew once you arrived things would change but your arrival would also signify I was on the correct path."

"I feel very honored to be here and I have learned so much in such a short time. Thank you for your hospitality and please let me know if I can do anything to help you in your journey."

"I will not be in this world much longer, I was afraid I might die before you arrived. Now that your have come I can pass into the next realm with peace and happiness. I saw your ride earlier. That was a very impressive display of your abilities. I know someone with your skills will be a fine guardian for my son."

"I will watch over him and do my best to keep him safely on his path."

"Thank you. I know it is time for you to go so please take this and remember. You will always have a home in Lhasa."

She placed a white scarf around my neck and kissed me on the forehead. With that our tea was over and she was escorted away by the monks. I walked back to the bell and the pool where I found my friend. He too had a scarf for me. As I stood staring into the pool I began rubbing Charlie's collar. The last sound I heard was the ringing of the bell in the courtyard.

Finding Catherine

"Welcome back stranger." Dad said looking up from his newspaper.

"Have you been sitting there since I left?"

"Pretty much, when you didn't come right back I figured it would be a little while so I set up a baby monitor. That way I could hear if something happened while I was in the house. Charlie has camped out here ever since you left. I made him a bed so he didn't have to lay on the cold floor but other than a few trips outside he has been patiently waiting."

"Anything else happen while I was gone?"

"The Major left a message on your phone saying he wouldn't be back until late this evening so he wouldn't be able to see you until tomorrow."

I was relieved to hear that. The last thing I wanted was him showing up early.

"Hey what happened to that silly dress and where did you find your Stanford sweatshirt?"

"Funny thing happened on the way to Abe's. The coordinates got changed on the transporter and I ended up, well right here. This shop, your shop, the other dimension you, father of Catherine Beaven. The Catherine Beaven that lost Charlie. The Catherine Beaven who along with her father invented Charlie's collar. The Catherine Beaven who is currently missing here in New Mexico."

"You really met the other me? Was I just like I am here or was I younger and more handsome?"

"Just like you are here but maybe a little smarter."

"Are you saying I'm the dumb Ben Beaven?"

"Sort of, I guess, yes you are definitely the dumber of the two. There I said it, are you happy?"

"No. So what did you learn?"

"A tremendous amount but before we do any more experimenting we have to find Catherine. I promised her dad that I would find out what happened to her and get her or whatever's left of her back to him."

"I hate to think of how worried he must be. What are we going to do to find her?"

"Let's start with what we know. Charlie was in the river so that means she was either in the river with him or near the river. No one has come to the ranch looking for Charlie so I have to assume she wasn't aware of where they became separated. She has her own transporter so she should've been able to get back home if it was working and she was okay. So again, I would have to assume either she is hurt or it is broken. She is very smart so if she isn't severely injured she should be making her way back here. That's what I would be doing if I were her. With all that in mind where do you want to start?"

"I'll start asking around the coffee shops and the grocery store. See if anyone has seen you or someone they thought was your sister anywhere I know you weren't. There is a free clinic down in the valley that she may have gone to if she needed medical help so I can check there tomorrow on my way to town. She needs to make some money too so why don't you check every diner and cafe down stream?"

"If it were me missing and someone said they'd look for me, would you be okay with them waiting until tomorrow when they were on there way to town or would you want them to get off the lazy duffs and find me now?"

"Since you put it that way. I'll get in the car right now. What are you going to do?"

"I'm going to check police reports, looking for any unknown females or unidentified bodies."

"How are you going to do that?"

"Remember I employ a hacker."

"Are you mad? You're going to send your assistant to look for the Catherine from the other dimension? Are you sure you can trust him that much?"

"No, but I guess I'm going to have to if it will help find Catherine."

Dad went off to check our list of most likely places Catherine would turn up while I went to Einstein's to see if I could find Kevin.

Kevin was sitting on the same bar stool I had found him on the other day. He had on the same shirt and I wasn't sure if he'd even showered.

"Kevin, what've you been doing, siting here for three days waiting for me to come back?"

"No, this is just a coincidence."

"Kevin you know I don't believe coincidence. Anyway it's hardly a coincidence to find you at Einstein's."

"I'm glad you haven't called but I was getting a little worried."

"Well I'm here safe and sound and I have a job for you. It's not official lab business and it doesn't pay but I still think you will like it."

"Where are we going to set up shop?"

"Dad's shop, grab your stuff and let's go."

"Right now?"

"Right now. This is very important."

On the way to dad's I did a little vetting of Kevin. I really wanted to trust Kevin but there were so few people who knew our security. If it wasn't Kevin that had breached our security then it was someone else I trusted. Kevin seemed to be as honest and trustworthy as ever and it came down to the fact that he had more to gain by helping me than he would've gained by sabotaging our project. Even if I regretted trusting him in the future he was my best hope for finding Catherine.

Once we were settled in Dad's shop I decided to start filling Kevin in on what I had been doing.

"So Kevin, I need your help but I don't have time to go into everything. I just need you to trust me and do what I ask."

"Have you swept this place for bugs yet?"

"No, I didn't figure anyone would consider Dad's shop."

"Before I start let's do a little housekeeping."

Kevin took my phone and my laptop and gave them a thorough check, he went over the entire shop until he was certain that there was nothing sending or receiving anything. He pulled out a small device from his bag and placed it by the window.

"What is that?"

"It will detect anything trying to listen from outside. If that alarm goes off start talking about baseball."

"Got it. So we are okay?"

"Yeah I think we're good now. Am I breaking any sort of laws talking about a classified event?"

"Yes. I think several"

"I thought so, just wanted to make sure."

"You know you are under no obligation to help me and any laws you break you are doing so of your own free will."

"Would you like me to sign something or can we get on with this."

"Sorry, I just hate dragging anyone into this mess but I really need your help."

"Catherine, relax, we're two of the smartest people around. I'm sure we can find a solution to any problem if we really put our minds to it."

"Well then let's start. Our problem is Catherine Beaven is missing. She has been missing for over a week now, she was last seen with her dog Charlie."

"Wait, you are here and so is Charlie so when were you missing for a week and why are you talking about yourself in the third person."

"I said Catherine Beaven is missing. I did not say I was missing. We are not the same person."

"There is another Catherine Beaven?"

"Yes, several I would imagine."

"I think I'm going to need more of an explanation."

"I will explain later. Right now I'm telling you what you need to know. You don't need to understand the how. Can you do that?"

"I think so. So to recap, Catherine Beaven went missing a little over a week ago with Charlie."

"Yes. Charlie was found in the River near the ranch and Catherine has not been seen since."

"Okay I need basic information about Catherine, height, weight, age, all that stuff."

"Kevin, genetically Catherine Beaven and I are the same."

"But she is not you?"

"No."

"But you are genetically the same?

"Yes."

"You will explain this all at some point, right?"

"Absolutely, but right now I need to find her as quickly as possible."

"Your DNA information is on file with the lab. I can take that and search all morgues and hospitals for Jane Doe's. Next I'll check for any police reports for any unknown female."

"Check burglary reports for the theft of women's clothes."

"Good idea"

"I'm going to go to the ranch to get a horse. If I ended up in the river I would head back here. The fastest way to do that would be up the canyon past the Puye cliffs. I'll call the pueblo Governor and let him know I'm on a search and rescue mission. I think that'll get me access. They are always very helpful if you just ask."

"By the time you get back I should have some answers."

"I won't make it all the way today. I'll have to spend the night on the mesa. My phone should work once I get on top of the mesa. Text me anything of importance. Dad will be back in a little while. Follow up on anything he finds. If you find her, don't try to contact her until I get there. It's very important that I am the one who talks to her first."

"Are you sure it's a good idea for you to spend the night on the mesa alone?"

"I won't be alone I will have a horse and Charlie. With all the things going on right now, riding a horse up the canyon is probably the safest thing I can do. Kevin, don't worry, I'll be fine. Just find Catherine. If she isn't in any of the places you are looking then she has to be in the canyon. I just don't know why she wouldn't have made it here by now. Even walking she should've been her a couple of days ago."

Charlie and I headed for the ranch. I camp out on horseback fairly regularly so it didn't take me long to gather up my stuff, saddle up Jasper and head for the canyon. I called the Governor on my way over and he was very helpful. We made a plan that I would leave my truck and trailer at the gas station and he would have someone drive it up and leave it at my Dad's. I promised to be respectful of the land and stay away from the sacred sights near the Puye Cliffs. He offered to send someone with me but I told him I would make better time if I went alone. Within the hour Jasper, Charlie and I left the truck and were headed up the canyon. I had chosen Jasper because he is a mustang. And for this job he would be perfect, small, sturdy and best of all barefoot. His bare feet wouldn't damage anything on tribal land and unless you were an expert tracker we would be very hard to follow. I rode up the first small mesa to get a better look at the river and where I had found Charlie. There was a good-sized arroyo that emptied into the river just down stream from the ranch. If Catherine had come out on this side of the river the easiest path would have been to follow that arroyo up into the canyon. I rode Jasper down into the arroyo and toward the river for a short way to see if there was any sign of anyone walking on foot. Unfortunately the arroyo is traveled a fair amount by pueblo members so there were several sets of footprints in the arroyo. I turned Jasper toward the mountains and we began to follow the arroyo up. After riding for about an hour we had climbed several hundred feet in elevation and the arroyo was getting narrow and steep. I had been following two sets of footprints for a while. Maybe Catherine had some help, maybe someone was following her or maybe neither of the prints belonged to her. The footprints left the arroyo and headed into the trees. Jasper, Charlie and I followed them as far as we could then they were lost in the pine needles. Anyone up here would be looking for water and there were only a few places to find it so I gave up tracking and headed to the closest stock tank. Riding alone through the trees with the sun warming my back helped me forget about everything and just enjoy the ride. Jasper was a steady mount and he would let me know if there was anything or anyone out of place. For a short time my only job was to stay on top and stay at least semi-conscious. As my mind wandered, I thought of Abe and Doc Miller. I promised them I'd come back. I really intended to but I was so glad to meet Catherine's father and learned more about how dimensional travel worked. Now I just want to get Catherine home safe. My mind came back into sharp focus when Jasper stopped abruptly and snorted. He stood stock still with his ears forward and his eyes glued on something in the trees.

"Easy boy. What do you see?"

I scanned the trees for some sign of what Jasper had found. He had blown out his nose and taken a few deep breaths so he may not have seen anything yet but he could certainly smell something.

"Okay what is it boy. I can't find it. Do you want to go give it a look?" I asked nudging him gently forward.

Charlie was also on alert he wasn't barking just looking far into the pines. Jasper took a few steps forward then stopped again. This time he pawed at the ground. The Hair on Charlie's neck stood up. These were all signs of a predator.

"Okay boys how about we back up a few steps and give whatever is in there, a little space."

I backed Jasper slowly, neither of us taking our eyes off the trees in front of us. We backed off thirty or forty feet and started circling around the area to the right. Jasper never took his eyes away from the center of our circle. Slowly and quietly we walked sideways around our unknown guest. As we made our way around I caught sight of what appeared to be a bear hidden between the pines. It wasn't moving with us so I just let Jasper keep and eye on it until we got a little further away. Once we had circled around the bear everyone went back to their casual walking pace through the trees.

"Good dog Charlie. Thanks for not chasing that bear. Good boy Jasper thanks for letting me know he was there."

I gave Jasper a good rub on his neck and reached in my pocket and pulled out a piece of jerky for Charlie. I have always been a big fan of rewarding animals for good behavior and both of them behaved perfectly. We broke into a clearing where there was a large watering pond for cattle. It was nearly dry this time of year but there was still some water to be had. Jasper and Charlie didn't hesitate walking into the mud to get some water. I opted for the water in my canteen. I hoped I would pick up the tracks of our two mystery hikers. But with the amount of mud it was impossible to distinguish any tracks. After Jasper and Charlie had their fill we continued on. I rode around the water hole for a while looking for any sign of footprints but couldn't find anything. I decided to ride up a rock outcropping to see if I could see any sign of human activity. Most people wouldn't have walked, let alone ridden up this pile of rocks but Jasper was an all star mountain horse. He got us up to the very top and stood quietly with all four feet on different rocks while I took a good look around. Further up the canyon there were a few man made fishing ponds. That would be a good place to make camp for the night and the most obvious place Catherine would have ended up if she were walking. Jasper carefully and skillfully took us back down to the clearing. Charlie had waited for us in the clearing and he seemed to have an idea of which way we should go to get to the ponds.

"All right, you lead the way Charlie. Just keep us out of the scrub oak. It always tears my shirts." I instructed Charlie as we headed further up the canyon.

Jasper, Charlie and I weren't setting a blistering pace but we were going to get about twice as far as you would expect someone to get on foot. Someone who didn't know the area would travel even slower so I figured it would have taken Catherine at least two days and maybe three to get to the ponds. If she spent one day along the river before she started that would still mean I should be a good four days behind her. There hadn't been any rain in the past four days so there still should be some evidence if she did indeed come this way.

The top of the mesa has a commanding view of the entire river valley and the Sangre de Cristo's. The sun was getting low and I wanted to make it all the way to the ponds before dark. Off to my right I could make out the cave dwellings in the Puye cliffs. Pueblo members had been using those cliffs since around 900A.D. There is something very magical about this land, so I tried to tread lightly. As we a neared the first pond I caught the slightest whiff of a fire. There had been some devastating forest fires through here recently so it could have just been the wind crossing some burned logs but I was certain someone had a fire. When I talked to the Governor he said no one else should be up here so this was either very good news or very bad news. Jasper, Charlie and I stayed in the trees as we rode along the three ponds looking for any evidence of human activity. As we approached the third pond I caught another whiff of a campfire. This time I was sure someone had built a fire. I scanned the forest looking for the slightest wisps of smoke.

"There, over there behind that log. Jasper do you see it."

Jasper was locked in on the log. He knew something was there. He wasn't snorting or pawing so he didn't feel threatened by whatever was on the other side of the log. Charlie was sitting very still but the end of his tail was starting to wag.

"Who is it Charlie? Do we know them?"

I eased Jasper around the end of the pond and within a few hundred yards of the log. From here I could tell someone had gone out of their way to make themselves nearly invisible. I slid off Jasper and told him to wait. Charlie and I walked quietly around the back of the log. Just as we got around the uphill side, someone came out from behind the log. Jasper spooked at their appearance, which drew their attention away from us. This gave Charlie and I just enough time to jump the person from behind. As we fell to the ground Charlie started barking and licking the person all over.

Double the Pleasure Double the Fun

"Charlie, I thought you were dead."

"Catherine, it's you, I can't believe I actually found you." I stammered looking at what appeared to be my reflection.

"Who the hell are you? How do you know my name and what are you doing with my dog?" The other Catherine demanded looking very puzzled.

"I'm you, you're me. Same person different reality, this should make a lot more sense to you than it did to me."

"Wow, you really are me. Oh this is way too strange. Should we meet? Are we going to cause a paradox? Do you have any food?"

"In order, yes, this is strange. I think it's okay for us to meet. I don't think we can cause a paradox because this isn't a time thing it's a dimension thing and finally I have plenty of food but it just ran off with the horse. He'll be back he never goes far. Now, a few questions for you. Are you injured? Where is your transporter? What does Major Allen carry in his inside jacket pocket?

"In order, yes I am injured. My ankle is broken and I have a nasty cut on my head. My transporter is broken, and a small black bag tied with a red ribbon."

"Can I take a look at your ankle?"

"Sure, I have it immobilized pretty well and I have fashioned some crutches out of some cottonwood branches I found near the river. I've been making pretty good time considering. I figured a few more days and I would be in Los Alamos."

"Why on earth did you start up this canyon with a broken ankle? You could have gotten some help in the pueblo."

"I am here from another dimension, I have lost my transporter and my dog, I have a broken ankle and I've nearly drowned. I go to the clinic in the pueblo with no ID. They call someone, they fingerprint me and I'm you. How messy do you think that was going to get?"

"Fair enough, but walking up the canyon?"

"I couldn't risk anyone seeing me. I thought about hitch hiking but everyone that drives that road works at the lab or someone in their family does. This really seemed like the best option. I had twenty bucks in my pocket so I bought some ibuprofen, beef jerky and some water at the gas station and headed out. I see Charlie lost his collar too. I was really hoping I wouldn't have to build one of these from scratch. I don't know if I can even do it here."

I reached in my pocket and pulled out Charlie's collar.

"Why didn't you lead with that? I could be drinking bourbon with my dad by now?"

"First thing's first. This one won't work again for a few days. This one," I said pulling the new transporter out of my other pocket and handing it to Catherine.

"This one needs to be safety checked and you need to explain the Charlie factor before it can be used."

"You used the collar?"

"Yes, I didn't mean to the first time, then I meant to the second time but accidentally ended up with your dad. He's worried sick about you and that's why I'm up here searching for you. I promised I would bring you home one way or another. I just got back this morning so you're stuck here for a few more days or until the new transporter your dad and I made can be tested."

"I can't believe it worked for you. It shouldn't have. It is set for my DNA it shouldn't work for anyone but me."

"I am you remember."

"I didn't take that into account."

"So can you explain why Abraham Lincoln and you both have the same dog?"

"No. That's it, just no?"

"Charlie's collar is a little different than my necklace. It needed to work for all of us because it was our backup. His collar has three DNA profiles stored. Mine, Dad's and Charlie's, whereas my necklace just has Dads and mine. Possibly since you and I have the same DNA his collar is acting as a locator beacon for the missing DNA profiles."

"So no matter which dimension we travel to it is looking for Charlie's DNA?"

"And possibly Dad's. Since they are usually together it will be hard to determine."

"Okay, so the new transporter your father and I built, where will I end up if I use it?"

"I don't know. If you use it to travel to my dimension you should end up somewhere near my father and possibly myself. If you travel to another dimension, I have no idea where you will end up."

"Can we code the new transponder with Charlie's DNA also?"

"I should be able to once we get to your father's shop but not out here. I assume he has a shop. I should have everything I need to set this transporter up for you and to safety test it."

"I've seen your fathers shop and I think you will be disappointed when you see this one, but it should have everything you need if you can find it."

"I hired a company to organize my father shop and he has a shop maid that comes in twice a month to keep it looking like it does."

"That would be worth the money."

"It is. To change the subject did you say Abraham Lincoln has a dog just like Charlie?"

"Not only a dog just like Charlie, apparently a DNA match to Charlie that he also named Charlie. The really odd thing is I named your dog Charlie before I found his collar. That seems like a very odd coincidence."

"I don't believe in coincidence."

"Neither do I, so what's the explanation?"

"I think we'll need more data before we can form any reasonable hypothesis and that will have to wait until we get out of the wilderness."

"We should be out tomorrow. You can ride Jasper and I'll walk. We can leave first thing in the morning. We will be to the forest service road by ten or eleven. I'll have Dad pick us up and take you to the E.R. You should be able to pass as me. Get you fixed up and by then Kevin and I will have a plan."

"If we are spending the night, how about you find that horse and make us some dinner?"

"Pushy aren't you?"

"You would know."

Japer hadn't gone far and was enjoying some grazing. I unsaddled him where he was and set up my picket line. I would take him to water later then I would probably let him loose for the night. I had enough oats for tonight and tomorrow morning. He always came back for oats. I put my saddle in a garbage bag and stashed it under a fir tree. Then I carried the saddlebags and the tent back to Catherine's log. Catherine cooked while I set up a better camp. We enjoyed a fine meal of dehydrated beef stroganoff and tang. I had thrown in a couple of chocolate bars and as always, I had my flask so it wasn't long before we were both plenty relaxed and ready for bed. I took Jasper to water, fed him a few handfuls of oats, tied a bell on his neck and set him free for the night. I was always a little hesitant to set Jasper free since he was a mustang but he had always come back to me or at least he always came back to the oats. He was safer not being tied and we were safer with him out there too.

"Be a good boy Jasper and I'll see you in the morning."

Catherine was asleep by the time I got back from turning Jasper out. I wished there was some way I could get a message to her dad. I bet he wasn't sleeping very well tonight. With that thought I sent a text to my dad to meet us on the forest service road at eleven.

Just as dawn was breaking I heard Jasper's bell outside my tent.

"Good morning Jasper." I said emerging from my tent.

"I know what you want. Just a minute let me drop the food bag out of the tree."

I walked over to the tree where I had hung my saddlebags and lowered them to the ground. Jasper was nuzzling around trying to open them before I could get the rope out of the tree.

"You're not that hungry, just wait a minute. I'll give you all that's left after I take you back to the picket line."

I took Jasper back to the picket line. While he was eating I went ahead and saddled him up. One less thing I would have to do later. By the time I got back to the tent Catherine was up and had found the coffee.

"I'm so glad you're prepared. I've really needed a cup of coffee for a few days now."

"Well, drink up. I'll break down the tent and make sure the fire is dead so we can get moving quickly this morning. I can wait on breakfast if you can."

"I can wait all day for food but I really need this coffee."

"See if you can leave me a taste. I'll be nicer if you do."

I had the campsite cleaned up and Jasper packed in twenty minutes. Catherine had saved me a half a cup of coffee. I drank it while I went down and got Jasper. I offered him one last drink at the pond then it was time to get Catherine in the saddle.

"Now this may hurt a little." I warned her as we readied her to mount.

"I think its probably going to hurt a lot but once I'm up there I think this will be a lot easier than walking."

"I'm going to lead him so all you need to do is stay on top."

"Okay on three, give me a boost. One, two, three ooowww!"

"You all right?"

"Great, I'm up, now let's go"

There was an old road that led from the ponds up to the forest service road. It was blocked off so cars could no longer use it but it was easy traveling for someone on horseback. Catherine and I talked as we walked along. Even though we were the same person, our lives had not been the same so we had different views on many topics. We talked politics, religion, men all the things that you are never supposed to talk about. I learned a great deal about why I think the way I do and what caused me to form my opinions. By the time we reached the forest service road we had solved all the problems of the world and were the best of friends. The one issue we hadn't solved was the best use for the technology Catherine had created and I accidentally used. That was the questions we were working on when Dad found us.

"Well aren't you two a sight for sore eyes?" Dad said as he got out of the truck.

"Hey Dad, thanks for the pickup service. I'll hold Jasper if you can help Catherine down. She has a broken ankle."

"You really are my Dad aren't you?" Catherine said looking a little bewildered.

"Yes, no, sort of. How about you just wrap your arms around my neck and just let yourself fall this way. I'll catch you I promise." Dad instructed Catherine as he carefully got her off Jasper. He carried her to the truck like she was a little girl and gently placed her on the front seat.

"Thanks Dad" Catherine said sweetly.

"You're welcome. Now let's get you to the Doctor and you back to Kevin. He hasn't left my shop since yesterday."

We stopped at Dad's and swapped vehicles. I sent Dad and Catherine to the hospital first then I went to the shop to find Kevin. I wanted him to go back to the ranch with me. As soon as Kevin and I started for the ranch he started quizzing me on what was going on.

"You promised you would explain to me why there are two Catherine Beavens running around. So I think this is about as secure a place as any for you to start talking."

"I'm tired, dirty, hungry and worst of all I need caffeine and you want an explanation now?"

"Stop, get food, get coffee, wash up I don't care just explain to me who that woman was your father just took to the hospital?"

"All right, let's go back some. What did you see happen the day I disappeared?"

"Besides you vaporizing? Really nothing."

"Kevin, you saw lot's of things. Focus and tell me exactly what you observed."

"You're right. There was a lot going on. I try not to think about it because it was so traumatic but if I really think about it, you didn't vaporize, and you went out of focus."

"That's good, now what else do you remember? Go back a little further."

"I coded a virus into the electromagnetic field and all the metal started heating up. I made eye contact with you and you caught on very quickly as always. You helped your jarhead of a boyfriend figure out what was happening. You were looking at Charlie when I saw Major Allen remove a something shiny from his pocket I thought he was going to get rid of it but instead he made a fist around it. That's when Charlie started to whine. The soldiers were already overheating and I thought they might just drop those hot weapons. I looked over and it looked like the Major was going to hit you over the head with whatever he had in his hand while you were trying to free Charlie from his collar when you suddenly started to lose focus. The soldiers were distracted so I pulled the fire alarm and the entire place filled with Halon. When the smoke cleared Major Allen had subdued the soldiers and you were just gone. Charlie was singed around where his collar had been but other than that everyone was just fine."

"Go back to the Major looking as though he was going to hit me. What could have been happening? Why would he, have taken that posture if he weren't going to hit me? What was in his hand?"

"Geez Catherine I don't know, I was so stressed. I know the Major wouldn't knock you in the head but I swear that's what it looked like. What happened to those guys anyway?"

"They won't tell me. Did you come up with any theories on who our mole is?"

"No, but you mouthed to the Major that he had a mole, do you remember?"

"Yes, I remember, why?"

"Well, I thought it was odd that when you did that he smirked a little. Like someone who thought they were getting by with something."

"Kevin, are you sure?"

"Think about it, what did you see when you told him that?"

"Well, he certainly didn't seem surprised but considering the situation, it did seem like an obvious statement. If I really think about it he did seem to smirk a little but this is all very subjective."

"I'm not trying to suggest anything I just remember that look. As far as what he had in his hand I don't know maybe it was his insignias? He tossed his jacked and put on a lab coat to blend in. What did he do with all his military bling? Do they only have one set? If so, does he still have them?"

"Brass, they are made of brass. The piece of metal Dad pulled out of my head was brass. A small point of brass from, say an Oak leaf. No, I have known Tom for fifteen years and we have been together for over a decade. He has never raised a hand or even his voice to me. He wouldn't hurt me. We must have something wrong."

"Maybe he had some sort of plan to save you by hitting you in the head or maybe it happened as you were disappearing and he tried to grab you and save you."

"The thought of this is so depressing. I can't imagine being betrayed by the Major. Okay enough about that let's get back to the double Catherine problem."

I was about to explain Charlie's collar to Kevin when I realized that officer Martinez had just began following me again. I slowed the truck down and pulled off to the side. Officer Martinez continued past.

"Kevin can you drive a truck and trailer?"

"I guess why?" I need you to take my truck to the ranch I'm going to take Japer and I'll meet you there. Here, put my coat and hat on. Don't worry I promise you will be fine."

"Catherine, what are you going to do?"

"I just got the sudden urge for a ride. Don't worry about it. I'll meet you at the ranch"

I took Jasper out of the trailer and headed into the arroyo just off the highway. It would take Kevin a good twenty minutes to get to the ranch but I could do it in about the same amount of time on Jasper but we were going to have to swim the river.

My thought was I would be coming in form the other direction and if Officer Martinez is acting as a scout I may be able to see who he is scouting for.

Jasper is a great little horse. He isn't my fastest, especially carrying all my gear but what he lacks in speed he makes up for with heart. It wasn't long before we were to the river. I found a nice place just upstream from the ranch to make the crossing easier for Jasper. Reluctantly, he entered the river. The current was swift but my little mustang was strong and before long he was dragging us out on the other side. I was cold and wet but we were making very good time. Jasper and I headed for the South fence line of the ranch. It had the most cover and unless you were looking for us we could probably ride right to the house without being noticed. As we approached the house I could see we had company. There were two dirt bikes parked in the driveway just below the house where no one would be able to see them. That was how they're getting on and of the ranch without being seen. I ran Jasper all the way to the pump house where I formulated my plan. I gathered my courage and headed straight up the driveway towards the motorcycles. I stopped briefly at the motorcycles and cut the cap off the spark plug wire with my Leatherman. Then Jasper and I headed for the house. I was questioning the safety of what I was about to do but as usual I decided, "What the hell" is usually the right answer. I rode Jasper right up onto the porch and through the front door.

As soon as I could stop Jasper I turned him around and ran him right back out the door and to the motorcycles. Being on horseback was a huge disadvantage in the house but out here in the open I had the upper hand.

Two men dressed completely in black ran out the back of the house and were just reaching the motorcycles when Jasper and I came thundering up. Due to my little sabotage job on the way to the house their bikes wouldn't start. This gave me enough time to run Jasper right over them and there bikes. I didn't want to give them enough time to draw a weapon so Jasper and I turned right back into them this time I had my rope ready. I am a lousy with a rope but I keep one on my saddle because they come in handy on a ranch. I really wasn't sure if I could actually rope these guys but I could keep them running until Kevin arrived. I knocked one of them to the ground as Jasper and I went by and miracle of miracle's I actually roped the other one. I dallied off hard and tight to the saddle horn and told Jasper to hold him. As I jumped out of the saddle hoping I could disarm the man I had just roped when I heard the most unpleasant sound. Right behind my head someone had just cocked the hammer of a pistol.

Shit! This is going to suck.

I began raising my hands slowly and turning around. Just as I faced my captor I let out a scream and stomped my foot. This caused Jasper to spook turning right into me, knocking me to the ground, running over the top of my captor and dragging the other man screaming behind him down the driveway. As I stood up I kicked the weapon that was lying in the driveway away and was about to unmask my assailant when I felt a burning jolt of electricity course through my body. As I fell to the ground and the world faded to black I looked into the eyes of the man who had just tazed me. Blue with a gray ring.

That's where I have seen eyes like that before....

Never Taze a Cowgirl

"Hello Catherine, I'm Doctor Romero. I've just had a good look at your X-rays and it appears that you have inline fracture of your Tibia just above your ankle joint. It is a nice clean fracture that should heal quickly. We will get you casted and set up an appointment with an orthopedist next week to have it checked. Is there anything else I can do for you today?"

"No, thank you Doctor. I would just like to get home where I can relax as soon as possible."

"We will have you out of here as soon as we can. Just promise to get some rest and take it easy when you get home."

"I Promise."

Catherine and Dad managed to get in an out of the ER and back to Dad's without crossing paths with anyone form the Lab. Dad found Catherine some clean sweats, helped her get cleaned up then insisted she rest until I returned. It had been a very difficult week for her and once she was clean and warm she fell sound asleep. Charlie curled up behind her knees to keep guard over her.

After an hour or so Dad started to wonder where Kevin and I had gone. He called my cell phone, which went straight to voicemail, then he tried Kevin's again no answer. Next was Major Allen, finally someone answered the phone.

"Hey Major, have you seen Catherine today?"

"No, Sir I haven't. I got in late last night and I've been in the office all morning. Is everything okay?"

"I'm sure it is but she was supposed to be here about an hour ago and I can't seem to reach her."

"Was she coming from the ranch or her lab?"

"She should've been coming from the ranch."

"I'll check on her and get back to you. Don't worry Sir, I'm sure she has just left her phone at the house and lost track of time in the barn."

"You're probably right. I am just still a little jumpy after the last time she went missing."

"Understandably so, Sir. I'll call you as soon as I have her in my sights."

"Thanks Major, I'm sorry to be a bother."

"You're no bother Sir."

Major Allen was out of his office and on the phone with the helipad as soon as he hung up on Dad.

"I need a chopper ready in five minutes." He demanded.

"Authorization? Whose authorization? Mine you paper pushing moron. This is a matter of national security and possibly life and death. Get me a chopper and a pilot."

The Major was on the helipad in less than five minutes impatiently waiting for the pilot to finish his pre-flight check and for the ground crew to finish fueling.

"Can we get going?"

"Sure we can go but until I'm finished with these checks and they finish fueling I can't guarantee how long we can stay up!" The pilot replied.

The Major climbed in and adjusted his headset; the pilot was quick to follow.

"As soon as they finish fueling we will be on our way."

"I thought these things were supposed to be fueled and ready to go."

"We had a flight this morning so we need to re-fuel."

"How much longer?"

"They just finished. Where to Sir?"

"There is a ranch down along the river just off to the north of the mesa."

"Right, I know which one we'll be there in five."

"How do you know which ranch I'm talking about? Have you been asked to fly there before?"

"No, Sir. We use it as a landmark to know where to make our turn up the canyon, Sir."

The Major didn't reply he just stared intently out the window in the direction of the ranch. In a matter of minutes the ranch was insight.

"Do one low pass over the barn and the truck and trailer, then turn up the hill towards the house."

"We'll do Sir."

Jasper was standing in front of the barn still saddled and someone was lying on the ground by the truck. In the driveway near the back of the house there was another person lying face down in the dirt.

"Set it down! Set it down now! Leave it running, this doesn't look good." The Major instructed the pilot

"Do we need backup?"

"Maybe, just watch for my signals."

"Be careful sir."

Major Allen was out of the chopper and running to the person face down in the driveway before the pilot had a chance to completely land.

"Oh God! You damn well better be alive."

"Or what? You'll kill me?" I said trying to smile

"What happened to you?"

"How about not yelling, tell that guy to shutdown the chopper and help me up."

The Major turned to the pilot and gave him the signal to kill the engine, while he helped me stand up.

"Catherine, who is lying by the truck?"

"Oh Shit! Kevin!" I said trying to run to the barn.

"Hey, how about you let me go check on him? You aren't in any condition to help anyone right now."

The chopper pilot had just jogged up. He helped me sit back down while the Major ran down to the barn.

"I need to find Jasper."

"Who is Jasper?" The pilot asked.

"My horse, he's a little dun Mustang."

"He is standing in front of the barn. Looked like he was waiting for someone to unsaddle him."

"Good boy Jasper. Can you give me a hand with him?"

"Shouldn't we wait for the Major?"

"Jasper needs to be unsaddled whether Kevin is dead or alive so we probably better get to it."

"Are you always this pragmatic?"

"I'm worse when I have a headache, and man do I have a headache."

"That happens when you get tazed."

"So I'm finding out. How did you know I was tazed?"

"You were face down in the dirt with no apparent injuries, I just assumed that's what happened."

The pilot and I walked to the barn where we found the Major and Kevin. Kevin was very much alive but not feeling very well. He had been tazed also.

"Hey Kevin, I found 'em." I said with a halfhearted smile.

"Yeah, me too. Any idea where they went?"

"Away?"

"Yeah, that's what I thought. How long did it take them to taze you?"

"I had them on the run for a while. I even managed to rope one of them. Last I saw of him Jasper was dragging him off down the drive. That's about the time the lights went out in my world."

I walked over and started checking Jasper for any injuries then led him into the barn where I started unsaddling him.

"Bastards cut my rope." I said as the Major walked into the barn.

"You're lucky that's all they cut. Can you tell me everything you remember?"

"In a minute let me take care of Jasper first."

"Catherine, forget the damn horse!"

"Listen here Major Allen! If it weren't for this horse I would probably be dead. Now why don't you get the hell out of my barn, go get your G.I. Joes and find out who did this and why!"

"Sir, there is a radio call for you," the pilot said, trying to avoid eye contact.

"Go! You do your work and let me do mine. When my head has stopped hurting I'll be happy to fill in any of the blanks you aren't smart enough to figure out."

"Attacking my intelligence? They really left you in a fine mood didn't they?"

"No, they didn't. You were supposed to look into this a week ago, so it's you I'm angry with. It's you I blame for nearly getting poor Kevin killed and it's you I expect to find these bastards and make them pay. I will tell you one thing, one of them has one hell of a rope burn, and more than a little gravel in his back."

The Major and the pilot turned and left the barn.

"CALL YOUR FATHER, HE'S WORRIED SICK," the Major yelled over his shoulder as he left.

As I unsaddled Jasper I could feel the tears start down my cheeks. I was shaking so hard I couldn't unfasten my latigo. I laid my forehead against Jaspers neck and cried. I stood there for quite awhile and sobbed into Jasper's mane before Kevin interrupted me.

"Catherine, your Dad want's to talk to you." Kevin said, handing me his phone and walking away.

"Dad, it's not a good time, I'm fine and we'll talk soon."

"You're crying, which means you're mad. Major Allen is mad too, do you think you two can stop bickering for an hour or two so we can take care of our other little problem that is sound asleep on the sofa with a broken ankle?"

"Right, I haven't forgotten about that it's just there was an incident here on the ranch. Forget about it, I'll be there as soon as

I can in the meantime just stay in the house please. I have to go, I'll talk to you soon."

Major Allen was walking back as I hung up the phone.

"Smother Dad with security. Do you hear me? Right now I want him surrounded, and whatever they do, don't let them go in. Preferably don't let him see them until I can get there."

"Yes, Ma'am. Your father will be protected."

"Thank you." I said trying again to unfasten my latigo.

"Can I help you with that?" Major Allen said in his sweetest voice.

"I'm scared, hurt and mad. You should probably just keep your distance."

"I'm scared and I'm mad. I thought you were dead when I saw you from the helicopter. Please let me help."

"Thanks."

Major Allen unfastened the latigo and finished unsaddling Jasper.

"Are you ready to talk?"

"Not yet, let's get Kevin and the pilot out of here then we can talk."

"I'll walk Kevin back to the chopper while you turn Jasper out. I don't want anyone in the house until my investigators get here but we can sit down here at the barn and talk."

Kevin and the pilot wandered in about then.

"Ma'am, Sir, I've been requested to bring both of you to the lab." The pilot said.

"I should stay here to protect the scene until my investigators arrive. Why don't you take Catherine and Kevin and I'll follow as soon as I can."

"If you insist Sir. Ma'am, Kevin, are you ready?"

"Go ahead, I'll be right there. The Major and I have one more item of business to go over."

"I'll have the bird ready for takeoff as soon as you're ready."

As soon as the pilot and Kevin left the barn I put my arms around Major Allen.

"I just need a hug."

"I didn't see that coming but okay." As soon as the Major wrapped his arms around me I unholstered his gun and pointed it directly at his liver.

"Catherine, what are you doing?"

"Major you better have some real good answers for my questions or I swear I will blow a 9mm hole in your liver."

"Catherine, you need to put my weapon back in its holster before one of us gets hurt."

"Major, Your weapon is chambered and ready to fire. Do you want to risk moving right now?"

"Fine! Ask your questions Catherine."

"First lace your fingers behind your head and get on your knees."

The Major complied, never taking his eyes off mine. As soon as he was on his knees I took two steps back.

"How long have you known the pilot who flew you here?"

"I had never seen him before today."

"Where did he come from?"

"I don't know, they rotate those guys in and out of here with some regularity."

"Think very hard Major, have you ever seen him before toady?"

"Catherine, I don't understand why these questions need to be asked at gun point."

"Answer the question Major!"

"I can't remember ever seeing him before to…oh my God! He was one of the soldiers who were in the lab the day you disappeared. He was the one Charlie peed on."

"He was also the son of bitch who tazed me!" I said lowering my weapon.

"I needed to see your reaction. Someone is lying to me and I had to make sure it wasn't you. Really sorry about that."

"Can I get up now?"

"As much as I love to see you on your knees, yes. Please get up."

"What do you want to do about Kevin and the pilot?"

"If it's not you, then the odds on Kevin just went up. I say we let the pilot take him back to the lab. If he is part of this nothing will happen to him. If he isn't, they may hold him hostage and oops, my bad."

"You know some people may consider you a psychopath."

"No, I don't enjoy doing this, I'm just willing to."

"We will discuss your willingness to point a loaded gun at me later, right now I would like do my own reaction check on that pilot."

"Fair enough let's go see how willing he is to leave without me."

"How can you be sure he is the guy who tazed you? If he thought you could ID him, he would have never let you see him again."

"His eyes, they are blue with a grey ring. Just like Abraham Lincoln's."

"How could you possibly know that?"

"History buff." I said with a shrug. I had a lot to explain to the Major but this was not the time.

As we neared the helicopter, Major Allen's investigators arrived. They had their work cut out for them but if there were any shred of evidence left behind they would find it. I stayed close to the investigators while the Major went over and talked to the pilot. I couldn't hear the conversation but the pilot seemed to get a little nervous. Then he flew off with Kevin.

"I sure hope you are right, and Kevin is somehow involved because if he isn't, I think they may do more than taze him the next time."

"I'm really not sure what to hope for. If I'm right, Kevin is a traitor, if I'm wrong I may have just sent Kevin to his death. All I really want is to go see Dad and make sure he's okay."

"Let me get these guys started and I'll drive you up there."

"I can take myself. I was tazed, not shot."

"I am not letting you out of my sight until I have everyone responsible for this locked up where I can see them."

"So how is it you didn't recognize that pilot from the attack on the lab?"

"They were all wearing masks remember?"

"You didn't take his mask off after you took him into custody?"

"By the time the smoke had cleared and I had restrained everyone and accounted for all the weapons. Half the security forces from the LANL were streaming in the doors. The D.O.D boys carted them off and I never saw them again. I read the reports and the transcripts of the interviews but I never actually saw any of their faces. When you had my Glock jammed into my side I did exactly what you said, I thought real hard about that mans face and I remembered his eyes. I remembered the way they looked at Charlie. I just really want to know how it is he is not behind bars?"

"If he's back here in uniform then the entire security force is in question. That's the same security force you sent to protect Dad, and Kevin knows about the shop. We need to get to Dad! What about the guys going over my house?"

"Do you have anything that may be of use to them?"

"Not in the house."

"Good girl."

The Major had a few words with his men and then we were off to check on Dad. I had tried to call him several times with no answer. I knew standard protocol in a situation like this would be to jam all communications, but it still worried me.

"Stop at the barn would you?"

"Remember, we're in a hurry."

"Stop at the barn!"

"Just wait right here this will only take a minute."

I ran into the barn and into my workshop. Behind some tools was a panel in the pegboard. Inside the panel I had a small wall safe. I quickly removed two flash drives and a small metal box and headed back to the car.

"That was quick."

"Just needed to make sure I had the electric fence on."

"You're a lousy liar."

"You're a worse spy."

"What's in the box?"

"My sex tape, wanna watch."

"You could have just told me 'none of your business'."

"You could have just respected my privacy."

"Say's the woman willing to brandish a fire arm to 'see my reaction'."

"Are we going to fight or are we going to check on my father?"

"I think we can do both."

"I said I was sorry about the whole gun thing."

"'The whole 'gun thing' as you put it was you ramming loaded gun into my liver and threatening my life! 'Sorry, my bad' comes up a little short."

"Well you weren't the only one held at gunpoint this morning, ya know."

"No. I don't know! You still haven't told me what happened this morning. All I know is that you were face down in the dirt when I found you, and you looked like you had been on the loosing end at the rodeo."

"I will explain everything but first I need you call the local yokels and ask for officer Martinez. I don't suppose you noticed his badge number the other night."

"I did notice, why do you want to talk to officer Martinez?"

"If I'm right, there is no officer Martinez with that badge number."

Within moments Major Allen had the local police department on the line, confirming my suspicions. They had more than one officer Martinez but none with that badge number.

"These guys are very well organized and very well funded. I am beginning to wonder if you shouldn't just give them what they want."

"I really wouldn't mind abandoning my research but I have a feeling if I do I may meet with an unfortunate accident. The only way I see to get out of this unharmed is to go public with my project. It's one thing to make a scientist disappear it's a whole other kettle of fish to make a world renowned, freed us from the industrial age, kind of scientist disappear."

"I think you may be right, but how on earth do you propose to reach that level of notoriety before they manage to destroy your work or worse, you?"

"Joe, Joe Casabona."

"Who is Joe Casabona?"

Gone But Not Forgotten

"Catherine, Catherine, you need to wake up."

"I'm sorry Sir, It's just been a really long couple of days"

"No need to apologize I just need to get you somewhere safe." Ben said in a near whisper.

"What's wrong, what has happened? Where is your Catherine?"

"Just take it easy. I don't know what has happened. I sent Major Allen looking for her and Kevin and I still haven't heard from them. I've just noticed some strange vehicles passing by the house and I think we may be under surveillance. I don't suppose you've seen Charlie's collar?"

"I haven't." Catherine said. Realizing they were probably being listened in on. She reached in her pocket and pulled out Charlie's collar and her broken necklace, showing them to Ben. Catherine had given her the collar on the mountain with specific instructions that if anything went wrong she was to use it to get back to her father.

"I see, maybe I left it in the shop."

"If you're going to the shop can you get something for diner out of the freezer?" Catherine mimed a screwdriver, hammer and an electrical meter.

"I'll be right back. Why don't you and Charlie do a little work on that puzzle?"

"If I can find that one piece I think everything else will go together real easy."

As soon as Ben left for the shop, Catherine began taking her broken necklace apart. She had designed it to be tamperproof but she had also had the foresight to enable her necklace and Charlie's collar to be linked together to provide extra energy for an emergency exit. This would mean she would have to leave Charlie but if she were going to abandon Charlie anywhere this seemed like the place. As soon as Ben returned with the tools she needed she could be on her way back to her dimension and her father.

"Charlie, come here boy. I may have to leave you here for a while do you think that will be okay?"

Charlie responded with a quick lick and a wag of the tail.

"I didn't think you would mind to much."

"Mind what?" Ben asked returning from the shop.

"Staying here, with you. I won't be able to take him home."

"Charlie is welcome to stay with me as long as you need him to." Ben said handing over all the tools.

"Thanks, I think that just might be the piece to the puzzle I need."

"How about I make us a drink?"

"Do you have any Pappy Van Winkle's?"

"That's the good stuff."

"Yes, so do you have any?"

"I think I may be able to find a child's portion for you."

"That would be perfect. I think we will be able to celebrate real soon." Catherine said attaching the leads from the electrical meter to Charlie's collar.

Just then there was a knock at the door. Catherine dropped her necklace in her pocket and put Charlie's collar back on him. Carefully concealing the electrical leads she had just attached.

"Coming," Ben said handing Catherine her drink and covering her cast with a blanket. It was Kevin at the door but he was not alone.

"Kevin, so nice to see you. Who is your friend?" Ben asked as Kevin and the pilot walked in.

"He is not exactly a friend Sir. I'm real sorry but he made me bring him here."

"It's okay Kevin why don't we sit down and we can talk about this."

"Listen pops, we aren't going to hold hands and sing Kumbaya. I need you to call your sweet little scientist daughter and have her meet with my employer. If she does that, you and geek boy here will live happily ever after. If she fails, refuses or pulls another one of her stunts. I will kill both of you and she'll still have to give us what we want." The pilot stepped out from behind Kevin to disclose the gun he had been holding against Kevin's back.

220

"Why would he need to call me I'm sitting right here on the sofa with my dog."

"That's impossible, I just left you on your ranch."

"Are you sure?"

"That was her at the ranch wasn't it geek boy?"

"I thought so."

"If you have double crossed me you geeky little bastard I swear I'll shoot you right here."

"Double cross him Kevin, that sounds a lot like you have already crossed me."

"You're not you, you're the other Catherine. The one Catherine was trying to find earlier."

"What are you babbling about you nerd? Who did I taze and leave at the ranch?"

"Yeah Kevin, who did he taze and leave at the ranch?" Ben asked trying to stir things up.

"You see there are two Catherine Beavens. They have the same DNA so you can't tell them apart. Catherine was going to explain everything to me on the way to the ranch but she spotted your stupid guy in the cop car and then everything went all pear shaped."

"So what you're trying to tell the handsome, yet none to bright man waving a loaded gun around, is that there are two people running around town with the same DNA and only you know this, there is no way to verify this and he should trust you? Did I get that right?" Catherine asked trying to keep the conversation spinning.

"No, yes, well you make it sound like I'm trying to hide something from him. I'm telling the truth and you know it and so does he." Kevin said pointing at Ben.

"I have no idea what's going on. You say you tazed my daughter on her ranch yet here she sits on the couch with her dog, where she has been all morning. I don't know who Kevin was with at the ranch but it certainly wasn't her and if you have any doubts about that you should check with all those men out there who have been watching this house all day."

"What men?" The pilot asked obviously very concerned.

"They aren't with you? I thought Kevin must have requested them. He has been working in the shop for the past two days on something. I just assumed they had something to do with that."

"You little traitor!" the pilot said hitting Kevin on the back of his head with his gun.

As the pilot drug Kevin over to the sofa he realized Catherine was gone. Charlie was sitting in the very same place and the blanket was lying on the sofa but Catherine was just gone.

"Where did she go?" the pilot demanded.

"Honestly, I don't know." Ben replied looking at the empty sofa.

"I'm going to give you to the count of three to tell me what the hell is going on here."

"What are you going to do after you get to three or is that as high as you can count?"

"Listen old man, I'm running out of patience. Where did she go?"

"I don't know but I think you may want to turn around."

"I said stop screwing with me! Now tell me where she is!"

"You thick headed bastard, the man said turn around!"

Major Allen and Catherine were standing in the doorway. Behind them were a dozen security officers with weapons drawn.

"That's impossible, you were just sitting on the sofa. You were wearing different clothes but you were just sitting there with you dog."

"Drop your weapon and get on your knees."

"See it's fine when you say that but when I say it we have to fight?"

"Catherine, take your father and Charlie to the kitchen."

"Yes sir. Come on Dad let's have a drink."

"I just had one but I think I could use another."

Dad and I sat in the kitchen and drank while Major Allen dealt with Kevin and the pilot. Dad told me how Catherine had used Charlie's collar to jump-start her transporter and he had kept the pilot and Kevin focused on him while she just disappeared.

"So Charlie still has his collar?" I asked.

"I think so check and see."

I gave Charlie a quick check and found his collar still had the leads attached but seemed to be fine.

"What are you going to do with that?"

"Nothing, who would think to check the dog?"

"Good point. Have you told the Major about the collar?"

"Not yet. One crisis at a time. The very odd thing about all this is these people are after my energy work. Can you imagine what they would do if they knew about the collar?"

"So how are you going to stop this? It doesn't appear they are the types to quit and go home."

"No, they will keep this up until they eventually get what they want. If they managed to corrupt a good kid like Kevin they are true professionals."

"Do you have a plan?"

"Of course I have a plan Dad. Now will it work? Hard to say."

"Are you going to share?"

"Do you remember Joe Casabona?"

"Yeah, the guy who spells his name for you. C-A-S-A-bona."

"That's the guy. I'm going to have him set up a press conference for tomorrow. I will release my findings to the entire world. It will be open source knowledge so no one can own it or profit from it."

"Won't you lose your job for that?"

"Yep."

"Can't you go to prison for that?"

"Yep."

"Sounds like a great plan. How do I help?"

"I love you Dad. How can people wonder where I get my rebellious streak from?"

"What are you two lushes rebelling against in here?"

"Don't call my Father a lush. He has had a very difficult day."

"Did you pull a gun on him too?"

"Let it go man, let it go."

"You pulled a gun on the Major? Where did you get a gun?"

"It was his. That's part of the reason he is being such a pansy about it."

"Sir do you have any more of the bourbon?"

"As long as I have Catherine I have bourbon."

"Understood Sir, understood."

"Oh you poor unfortunate souls have to share your lives with mean old Catherine. I'll just take my dog and go home now."

"No you won't!" Both Dad and Major Allen said in unison

"What, you want to keep the dog?"

"We are all going to be spending some quality time together. I have lots of unanswered questions and both of you are under twenty four hour protection ordered by the D.O.D."

"Do you have a hot agent to look after Dad? Someone older than me but not too old?"

"I am looking after both of you personally."

"Awkward, I really don't want to know what the two of you do. I've spent years trying to avoid that mental image." Dad chimed in trying to get a rise out of the Major.

"I need to get in touch with Joe so we can set up a press conference."

"Do you listen? There will be no press conference, you are in protective custody."

"Do you listen? These people are not going to stop until I am dead. They have destroyed my research. The only reason they haven't killed me yet is they know they don't have all of my research."

"Your sex tape?"

"Whoa! Really would like permission to leave the room." Dad screamed covering his ears.

"It's not a sex tape. Relax Dad, I just said that to keep people from asking any more questions."

"I would still like permission to leave. I know how you two get and this is going to take awhile. Try not to break any dishes and I'm cutting you both off." With that Dad took the bourbon bottle and left the room.

"Major, you can't help me with this. I am going to break a boat load of laws and be subject to prosecution."

"Why? I'm sure there must be a legal way to do this."

"You know, you've said I am better at connecting the dots than anyone you've ever met. I'm telling you what I see. The only way I can connect the dots without ending up dead is to take away their incentive. If I go public with my research I will lose millions possibly billions of dollars worth of revenue for the Lab and our Government but I will give the people of the Earth a sustainable, renewable energy source and potable water. This will free us from the industrial age and allow us to move forward as a planet. I'm no martyr but my life is not more important than that."

"It is to me."

"No, it's not, you're just being greedy and selfish."

"How do I help?"

"That's the spirit. Keep Dad safe, set up a meeting with Joe and whatever you do, don't let Allison find out about any of this."

"Okay, consider it done. Now I need a complete explanation of why two people swear they saw you sitting on your dad's sofa when I know you were with me."

"Now?"

"Now!"

"Dad we're going to need that bourbon back."

Back to the Beginning

Everything was ready for the press conference. Joe and Catherine were the only two missing. Every one was starting to get fidgety when Catherine hobbled in.

"Good afternoon Ladies and Gentlemen thank you for coming. I am here to explain that as of today the world has a new renewable, sustainable source of energy. This announcement has been a long time in the making and a lot of people have risked their lives and their careers to make this announcement. Please listen carefully to what I have to say and please use your collective power as journalists to ensure my protection. In a few moments some men will be here try to stop this announcement, if you let them, they prevent the evolution of this planet."

With that Catherine turned to walk off stage.

"Catherine, what happened to your leg?"

"Long story, I really need to go."

"You can't go we don't have all the information."

"Everything you need is on the flash drive on the podium. Just put it in and let the program run. Whatever happens keep the program running. I really have to go. Please, my life depends on this."

Catherine began walking out of the press conference just as four gentlemen in black suits walked in. The computer presentation she had made was already playing in the background as she walked straight toward the men.

"What's wrong gentlemen you look like you've seen a ghost?" Catherine said making her way to the door.

"You need to come with us."

"I don't think so. I need to go home."

"Ma'am please, come with us."

"Do you see this room full of journalists? They are recording your every move so I think you are the ones that need to go."

"Catherine you need to stop this press conference and come with us." A voice said from behind the four men.

"Allison? You're the one behind this?"

"I'm the one arresting you for treason and other crimes against our country. Now this press conference is officially over."

"Ms. Carter is what we are hearing true? Has LANL developed a renewable sustainable energy source?" One of the reporters asked

"No, there is no truth to this Ms. Beaven has suffered a mental break. I am sorry for the confusion."

"If she has suffered a mental break why are you arresting her for treason?"

"Some of the information she is disseminating is considered classified and top secret. Now we really need to turn off the presentation."

"Ma'am there seems to be a problem we can't turn it off."

"Kill the power and clear this room!"

"Don't loose your cool Allison you're on National television."

"Catherine I don't know what planet you've been living on but nobody broadcasts a science press conference live."

"They do when it's hacked into one of our military satellites and broadcast over every frequency. Smile you're on candid camera. Go ahead and explain to the people of the world why you, as the Deputy Director of a science lab think you have the right or the power to keep this technology secret? Could it have anything to do with all that money piling up in your off shore accounts? Now if you'll excuse me I really must go."

Catherine walked out the front door passing Major Allen and his men as they entered the building.

"Catherine, what happened to your leg?"

"Really it's nothing, I promise it will be better by the time you see me again. Make sure you get those cuffs good and tight on Allison. She is very slippery."

Dad and Charlie were waiting just outside. Charlie gave a quick bark as Catherine got in the car and Dad drove off.

"Good boy Charlie. Thanks for the vote of confidence."

"So everything worked out as planned?"

"Thanks to your brilliant daughter. You know your planet will never be the same after today? She really has changed the world. Sorry she wasn't here to see it for herself."

"Any idea where she is?"

"According to the tracking device Dad, my Dad, put in her transporter, Tibet. Oh God I bet she really hates that stylist now."

"As long as she has her boots on she'll be fine. So would you like to stop for some ice cream?" Charlie gave a big bark

"Sure, I love ice cream."

"I'll buy if you tell me when the two of you cooked up this plan and how you knew it would work."

"We had no idea if it would work or not. But we had to end this stupid game of cat and mouse somehow."

"I still don't understand how you knew to come back?"

"When Catherine and I were on the mountain we went over everything that had been happening to her, from the attack at the lab to someone searching her home. It became clear that in order for her to be safe, this project had to become public knowledge. If she were going to do that someone would surely try to stop her. She told me she had all her data backed up and hidden. Since she didn't know who to trust she decided to move everything to your shop where no one could find it. When I disappeared from your sofa I didn't transport I just hid. You just assumed I transported."

"So you've been here all this time?"

"Yes, when Catherine brought the tools back to your shop she found me and that's when we devised our plan. In order to keep you and Major Allen safe I stayed hidden. Catherine just went along with your idea I had transported back."

"The two of you worked this whole thing up so there would always be one of you to make the announcement."

"Yep. It was my idea to stay and she thought of everything else."

"God, the curse of two genius daughters."

"So can I take a rain check on that ice cream? I would really like to go home."

"Of course you can sweetie. Tell your dad hello from me and maybe someday we'll get to meet."

"I'll be working on a communication component for the transporters. Something like inter-dimensional face time."

"Well, go on them. Godspeed Catherine, Godspeed."

For Whom the Bells Toll

With the temple bells still ringing in my ears, I found myself wondering about the press conference. It should have happened a few days ago. I hoped everyone was all right and I wonder how Joe had faired with the goons. As the world came into focus I was standing face to face with a very unsavory character.

"I've been expecting you," were the firsts words I heard as I appeared in my Fathers shop.

"Well, I certainly wasn't expecting you. Where is Dad?"

"Your Father is safe, don't worry. Now I think its time you come with me so you can explain your little disappearing trick to my boss."

"Can I change out of this dress?"

"No, maybe you'll be a little easier to deal with in that get up."

"All right then, take me to your leader. Oh where's the dog? Someone is feeding the dog, right?"

"The dog is with your dad and they are both being well looked after. We really don't want to hurt you or anyone else. If you cooperate you will probably end up a very rich woman."

"That would be a little easier to believe if you weren't pointing a gun at me."

"I wouldn't need the gun if you were a little easier to talk to."

"Oh sure, blame the victim."

"Victim, you are anything but a victim. I've seen you take down grown men with that sharp tongue of yours. You don't do anything you don't want to do and even with this gun I feel at a slight disadvantage. Most people either get lots of smarts or the ability to think on their feet. You have both."

"I'm touched, an admirer. Too bad you're a terrorist, but at least you can send me fan mail from prison."

"Terrorist is such an overused term these days. I'm a freelance military operative."

The man with the gun escorted me outside to a waiting SUV. There were two additional guards standing beside the SUV along with a driver.

"Four armed men just for me I feel so special."

"Ma'am, I don't know who you are or what you do but there are some very important people who have been trying to talk to you. They would've sent a hundred men if they needed to, so please this time, just cooperate."

"Are you the same guys from the restaurant? I thought I'd seen you before. And you, you riding shotgun, you are the guard from my lab. You totally blew it when you said hello. I would have never noticed you weren't the same guy if you had just kept your mouth shut. I bet you were the guys who did that really lousy black bag job on my house too. What were you looking for there anyway?"

"Ma'am I am going to ask you to just sit quietly until we get there."

"Son, you can ask me to sing the National Anthem if you want but I know and you know you are not allowed to hurt me so I feel safe enough even between these two military style bookends to ask as many questions as I'd like. If you choose to answer them great, if you choose to sit quietly, even better. I will not sit quietly between armed men who have just kidnapped me."

"Well, I had to ask. Okay boys, she's all yours."

The guard on my left pulled out a syringe from his pocket and jabbed me in the thigh, while the guard on my right handcuffed my wrist to his. The next thing I knew I was sitting in a very nice bedroom. I was sitting on the bed with my right wrist handcuffed to the bed. I was propped comfortably with several large pillows as though someone had taken great care to ensure my comfort while handcuffing me to a bed. As my eyes began to focus I noticed I was not alone in the room.

"Dad, Charlie, am I happy to see you."

"We're happy to see you too. Nice outfit, how was Tibet?

"How did you know I went to Tibet?"

"That tracking device Catherine's dad put in the transporter."

"Dad! We shouldn't be talking about that here and where did you get that scarf?"

"Your horse came in with it the other day and why can't we talk here?"

"Bad guys, guns, I'm handcuffed. Hey why aren't you handcuffed or anything?"

"I'm nice."

"Really? You are being nice to the terrorists?"

"Who said they were terrorists?"

"The guns were a hint. They kidnapped and sedated me and you don't think they're terrorists?"

"No, I'm pretty sure they aren't terrorists. They've been real nice to Charlie and me. Look at what a nice hotel we're staying in."

"Oh he didn't? You aren't, now I know why I'm handcuffed, so I don't beat the two of you to a pulp. I can't believe you are helping him with this."

"You had it coming."

"There are always consequences for your actions. You pulled a gun on me. What did you think the consequences for that would be?" Major Allen said calmly strolling into the room.

"You punked me? That's low for even you."

"That's a little harsh. You are still in protective custody. I was just ensuring your safety."

"And the handcuffs are to ensure yours?"

"Something like that. You are a hard woman to keep in one place."

"So I guess the press conference was a success?"

"Yes, we have arrested everyone involved and I'm working on a full pardon for your acts of treason."

"Right, I forgot about that."

"There is just one more item of business to wrap up and I think all of our questions will have been answered."

"Was it Allison?"

"Yes, but that's not the question I had in mind."

Major Allen reached into his pocket and pulled out the little velvet bag.

"Wait!"

"Wait? I've waited ten years."

"I know but there is one more thing I have to do and you might want to wait until I get back."

"What do you have to do and get back from where?"

"I think I figured something out in Tibet and I need to test my theory."

"How does this in anyway impact what I was about to ask?"

"You're my happy thought. It's like Peter Pan. I need that bag to stay in your pocket for just a little while longer."

"You are the most frustrating woman on the planet, what made me think this would work?"

"You love me and I love you and I promise if you wait for two days you'll have me for lifetime."

"Is that my reward or my punishment?"

"That's your choice."

"Okay, you have 48 hours but after that your little black bag of happy thoughts turns back into a pumpkin."

"I think you have mixed your fairy tales but I get it. I won't keep you waiting. Now un-cuff me so I can get started."

Major Allen released my handcuffs, kissed me on the forehead and turned and left the room.

"You don't deserve him!" Dad exclaimed.

"You're probably right."

"How could you break his heart like that? Why couldn't you just let him have his moment?"

"Dad, this is what I need to do. He understands that and I promise you both it will be worth the wait. Now I need you to take Charlie to Catherine for me."

"You need me to do what?"

"You heard me. Take Charlie's collar and the spare transporter and go to Catherine. In 48 hours I need you to set the transporter to 3H1R15. That should bring you straight to me. Make sure to bring Charlie's collar back with you and some warm clothes. Also I need you to give Catherine this note. She will understand what I need her to do."

"Where are we going?"

"Tibet."

"Why are we going to Tibet?"

You'll see when you get there. No get going so you won't be late."

I gave Dad and Charlie each a big kiss and stuck the note in Dad's pocket for Catherine and in a matter of moments they had faded out of the room. Next I sat down and wrote a letter to Major Allen. I gave him very specific instructions on how to find me in 48 hours. If he were my soul mate he would have no trouble finding me. Finally I focused my mind on breathing the clear high mountain Tibetan air deep into my lungs. As I breathed slowly and deeply I could hear the sound of the temple bell. The sound grew louder and louder until it suddenly stopped. I opened my eyes and found myself standing directly in front the monk that had been ringing the bell.

"Namaste Adoy." I said bowing my head.

Doppelgänger

Dad and Charlie arrived safely much to the surprise and joy of Catherine and Ben. Dad filled Catherine in on what happened after she left and gave her the note. She read it quickly and announced.

"Come on boys we have some work to do."

"What did the note say?" Ben asked.

"Catherine needs a transporter for Major Allen."

"Is that a good idea?"

"Probably not but I have to trust her, she really wouldn't do anything I wouldn't do."

"Major Allen tried to propose to her when she got back from Tibet but she stopped him cold in his tracks." Dad informed the group.

"Major Allen tried to propose?" Ben and Catherine asked simultaneously.

"Yeah and I felt real sorry for him when she stopped him before he could get that damn ring he's been carry around out of his pocket."

"She knew about the ring?" Catherine asked.

"Don't you?"

"Okay, so Catherine needs a transporter for Major Allen and you need to take it and Charlie's collar to her in less than 48 hours." Catherine said recapping.

"That's the plan."

"Well, we have a lot of work to do. You boys get started and I will call Major Allen, we're going to need his DNA."

Catherine called Major Allen and asked him to stop by her Dad's after work. The three of them spent the rest of the day working on building a transporter for Major Allen and improving the other transporters. They added the communication feature Catherine's had discussed earlier. Major Allen stopped by after work and was completely confused when he found two Ben Beavens working together in the shop. Major Allen, Catherine and both the Ben's decided that whatever Catherine was up to it must be very important and they would do anything they could to help her.

"She said you should all meet her in 48 hours?" Catherine questioned Dad again.

"Yes."

"How is she going to get anywhere? We have all the transporters?"

"I don't know? All she said was she figured something out in Tibet and she needed to test her theory. "

"Why does she need Charlie's collar? If she wanted to keep the dog I would have let her."

"I don't think she wanted to keep Charlie, she loved him but she wanted to make sure I brought him back to you so I don't know why she wants his collar."

"I'm still confused but I think I may know what she's up to. Let's quit for the night. I'm hungry my leg hurts and I'm sure we will have enough time to finish everything tomorrow."

"Major, why don't you take Catherine inside, make her a drink and get her to elevate her leg. Ben and I will clean up out here then make a pizza and beer run."

"That sounds perfect. I wanted a few minutes alone with Catherine anyway."

Major Allen helped Catherine into the house and got her situated on the couch. Charlie and Lucy curled up on the floor beside her while the Major mixed them some drinks.

"So did I hear correctly that my doppelgänger tried to propose and was shot down?" The Major asked from the kitchen.

"I don't think he was shot down but I think he may have been winged."

"Any idea why?"

"No, you met my doppelgänger, and I heard you made a pass at her. What do you think?"

"I think she loves him very much and whatever she is doing she has a very good reason for."

242

"Major Allen, are you a romantic at heart?"

"Yes I am and I think it's high time I prove it."

The Major reached in his pocket and pulled out the little velvet bag he had kept there for over a decade.

"Catherine Elizabeth Beaven, would you do me the honor of becoming my wife?"

"Have you asked my father?"

"Is that a trick question?"

"Yes, and yes I would be honored to be your wife."

A Heart's Desire

The courtyard was filled with monks in red flowing robes praying and chanting. Peter and Heinrich had built a small alter next to the reflecting ponds just as I had requested. The entire village was beginning to arrive dressed in their finest and most colorful attire. The gilded roof was glistening in the afternoon as I stepped out of my cottage with Charlie at my side. Once again young women had arrived at my door with silk, ribbons fine wool to dress me and braid my hair. This was my most beautiful outfit yet but I wasn't sure I would ever manage to take it off without their help.

"Are you ready Miss Catherine?" Adoy asked.

"Yes, I am ready. I have followed your instructions and I believe I am ready. Has my father arrived?"

"Yes he is with Heinrich and Peter. The monks have been praying since dawn, the entire village has arrived, you are radiantly beautiful, everything is as it should be."

"Thank you for everything, I can't think of a better way to do this."

"This is a grand path you have chosen Catherine and you are a grand woman. Open yourself completely today and all will be well."

"Or as we say in the west; Screw your courage up real tight and always trust your cape."

Adoy didn't understand my reference but the time had come to lead me to the altar by the reflecting pool. As they approached the altar I stopped and looked to the top of the stairs. The Dali Lama was watching from his gilded throne with his mother standing behind him. She looked happy today and at peace. I folded my hands and bowed my head in his direction then proceeded to the altar. Before I stepped onto the altar I removed my shoes and her socks as per Adoy's instructions. As soon as I was standing barefoot on the altar facing the reflecting pool everyone began a low humming chant. Adoy took his position by the bell and I focused on the one thing I wanted more than anything. Slowly in the ripples of the reflecting pool a shape began to take form. The shape became sharper and sharper until it a single horse with a rider could be seen. At the moment the image became clear Adoy began to ring the bell very slowly and very quietly. The reflection became sharper and sharper and the image moved from the back of the reflecting pool to the center. Adoy continued ringing the bell louder and louder, the chanting became louder and louder until suddenly the reflection was gone. Adoy stopped ringing the bell and everyone looked intently at the palace gate.

Across the courtyard I could see a single horse and rider approaching. The rider was dressed in full military dress; the sun was glinting off his sword with each stride. In a matter of moments the horse and rider had crossed the courtyard and were standing by the altar.

"You rang?" The Major asked with a smile.

"So to speak."

"You are the most beautiful woman I have ever seen and this is the most magnificent place I have ever seen." The Major said looking all around.

"I was hoping you'd like it. Thanks for showing up."

"Thanks for bringing me here."

"You're welcome thanks for trusting me and understanding what I wrote in my letter."

"That's right I came here to ask you something. Let me see if I can remember? Right, what do you think of my cavalry uniform?"

"I think it's lovely, what did the horse think about the sword?"

"She got used to it but I don't think that was the question."

The Major reached in his pocket and pulled out a small velvet box.

"What happened to the bag?"

"You aren't the only one who had 48 hours to get this right."

"And Dad was afraid I had run you off."

"Not a chance." The Major said sliding off his horse and stepping onto the altar. As he bent down on one knee he asked.

"Catherine Elizabeth Beaven, I have loved you since the first moment I saw you and I will love you as long as my soul goes on. Would you fulfill my heart's desire and spend the rest of your mortal days as my wife?

I knelt beside him and answered.

"Major Thomas Allen, I could not spend my life any other way."

Then he placed a small band of gold on my finger.

"This ring is fragile yet strong, it will bend long before it breaks and if cared for properly will last a lifetime, just like my love your you."

Suddenly everyone in the courtyard fell silent and knelt. The Dali Lama had walked down the temple steps and was standing next to Adoy by the bell.

Major Thomas Allen, does this woman please you? The Dali Lama asked walking toward the altar.

"Yes Sir." Major Allen responded starting to get up. As I quickly pulled him back to knees the Dali Lama spoke again.

"Miss Catherine, you are a very powerful soul. You have manifested your heart's desire. Can you be happy following his path?

"We share a soul, his path is my path and I will find true happiness with him."

The Dali Lama placed his small hands on both our heads. It felt as though we had been attached to a human battery. Everything seemed to glow and I was filled with amazing warmth.

"Major Thomas Allen, Miss Catherine your souls have been united and will seek each others company for the rest of eternity."

The Dali Lama walked off the altar and back up the steps to his golden throne. Once he was on his throne he clapped his hands and the party began. Dad had brought several bottles of bourbon, which made him the most popular man in the courtyard. Peter had brought the seamstress and they seemed to be getting cozy while Heinrich and Charlie made the rounds begging food and spreading joy. The Major and I snuck back to my cottage to figure out how to get me out of my dress and spend so much needed time alone.

Marital Time

I awoke to the sounds of giggling young women. I opened on eye and saw the girls that had dressed me the day before walking around the cottage picking up pieces of my dress. The Major and I had unwound and peeled away layers of silk leaving them strewn around the cottage as we went. I'm sure there was a more dignified way to remove my very beautiful garment but that had not been our focus last night. The girls gathered up all the pieces of my dress and left two fresh bundles of clothes along with some breakfast for us beside the fire. Charlie was already enjoying his yak milk.

"Good morning Mrs. Allen." The Major said pulling close against him under the covers.

"Oh my god! Is your mother here?" I said tickling his feet with mine.

"I didn't think that would fly but I thought it might sound nice this morning."

"It sounds wonderful this morning."

"This isn't real, I mean this didn't really happen. We are in some sort of altered state, right? We aren't actually in Tibet, I mean physically. What I'm trying to say is how the hell did I get to wherever I am and are we actually married."

"Having second thoughts already? This wasn't some quickie marriage at the Wee Chapel of the Heather in Vegas."

"How about we start at the beginning and you explain everything. I mean everything this time."

"I'll explain everything I can. There are some things I still don't understand. First throw a log on the fire, bring over that breakfast tray and our clothes then after breakfast I will tell you everything."

"How about I leave the clothes and just bring the food?"

"How about you remember my Dad is around here somewhere and that door doesn't lock."

"Maybe that'll teach him to knock?"

"Teach who to knock?" Dad asked walking through the door.

"Good morning Sir," Major Allen said grabbing a pillow to cover himself with.

"Good morning son, you know you should put some pants on before you tend the fire or one spark could put you out of commission for weeks."

"Good advice Sir, now if you could please excuse us my wife and I were about to enjoy some breakfast and some marital time together."

"Okay boys, Major come back to bed, Dad tell me what you came for then get the hell out."

"Major you need to be faster with the coffee. She's surly in the morning without caffeine."

"And surlier yet when people bother her. Now what do you need Dad?"

"Is it okay to give some of the village children rides on your horse?"

"Yes, of course. When your finished take her to the reflecting pool and ask Adoy to send her home."

"Can he do that with out a transporter?"

"Yep, now is there anything else?"

"What do you want me to do with Charlie's collar and Major Allen's transporter?"

"Leave them with me. As soon as yours is charged you can go back. Major Allen and I have a honeymoon to take. We'll be back in a few days."

"Okay, I'll leave you two to your 'marital time'."

"Thanks Dad and I love you."

"I love you both and I'm taking the dog. He needs to get out for some fresh air."

Dad and Charlie left leaving the Major and I to enjoy our breakfast in bed. I explained as much as I could to the Major about the transporters and the other Catherine and the other Ben. The most difficult part was explaining how he had ended up here without a transporter.

"In your letter you told me to go sit on your horse dressed in my best uniform and think about the thing I wanted most in life.

You told me to listen for the bell and follow the sound in my mind."

"And you did. You followed it to here."

"So 'here' is in my mind?"

"Well yes, but it's not just in your mind it is a real place."

"So I'm actually, physically in Tibet."

"Yes, but not the Tibet in our dimension, a different Tibet."

"Can we go home?"

"Yes, but first I would like to make one stop."

"You talk about this like it's train travel, can we just make a stop?"

"I don't know, I think so. I would like to try."

"Did the Dali Lama say our souls were joined for eternity?"

"That's what the man said. How about we get out of this bed and start our new lives together with an adventure?"

"I was transported to our wedding aboard your horse by chanting monks and married by the Dali Lama. That's not enough adventure?"

"That's just the beginning."

After the Major and I were dressed we headed down to the courtyard just in time to send my horse back home. Adoy was very pleased to see us and offered us a blessing on our marriage. I found Dad and Charlie and let them know we would be leaving but I would see Dad back at the ranch in a few days.

"As for you Charlie. I don't know when our paths will cross again. You take care of Peter and Heinrich.

Charlie wagged his tail jumped up and gave me a quick kiss on the nose then ran out of the temple and toward the village. I pulled Charlie's collar and Major Allen's transporter out of my pocket and set the coordinates. I gave Dad one last quick kiss, held Major Allen's hand and we faded away.

A Charlie of Her Own

"Catherine! I swear if we don't die I'm going to kill you for this."

"Relax Major, everything will be all right. Charlie will be here soon."

"CHARLIE, you're counting on a DOG to save us? And didn't we just leave Charlie in Tibet?

"Not that Charlie, my Charlie. If my theory is correct I should have a Charlie of my own."

"Catherine, look around? Please tell me how a dog is going get us out of here."

"I don't know Major, I just know he will. Just like I knew you would meet me in Tibet. I know Charlie will be here and everything will be just fine. Now, calm down, try to relax not so much you fall to your death and focus on Charlie."

"What about the bear?"

"What bear?"

The Major and I had arrived in a very precarious place. We were perched in a pine tree that was growing out of what appeared to be a shear cliff face. The top of the tree reached nearly but not quite the top of the cliff. While the base of the tree provided only enough room for one person to carefully stand. The view was stunning and I guessed we were somewhere in the Northern Rockies. I was trying to decide if climbing down the tree would enable me to climb up the cliff when the Major pointed out the bear. A North American Grizzly.

"Oh! That bear."

"Yes, Catherine. That bear. That very large Grizzly bear."

"Relax, if we can't get up that cliff he can't get down it."

"Are you sure?"

"Not at all, I was just trying to sound reassuring. Seriously I think we need to ignore the bear and focus on Charlie. Besides there isn't anything we can do about the bear."

"What if your theory is wrong?"

"You have a choice. Fall to your death or be eaten by a Grizzly."

"Let's hear it for Charlie."

"That's the spirit."

The Grizzly was pacing back and forth along the cliff trying to find a way to get to us. The Major threw a few pinecones at him, which only agitated him, more. I began unraveling my silk sash and braiding it into a rope.

"Hey Major, why don't you take your belt off and lash yourself to the tree. Just in case smoky bear comes down here he can't shake you out."

"Great advice! Have you seen Charlie yet? How much longer until comes and saves the day?"

"Ask and ye shall receive."

Charlie had just shown up on the cliff about hundred and fifty yards from the bear. He was with a handsome cowboy who had just leveled his rifle sights on the bear.

"See everything is going to work out. Charlie's here and he brought a gun."

"It's a rifle and we are still stuck in a tree on the side of a cliff."

"Whatever, we'll be down and headed home with Charlie in no time."

"You think that cowboy is going to give you his dog?"

"It's not his dog and I have his collar to prove it."

"Catherine please don't get us shot out of this tree.

"We are going to have the best honeymoon story ever."